SHE PITCHED FORWARD INTO HIS ARMS . . .

She was instantly caught and held, brought in against his body so that she grew aware of its hardness, even as he must have been aware of the softness of her own flesh. His arms closed about her and he held her crushed against him.

His kiss was firm, yet soft, and in it, Kai sensed the hunger in the man, the need he had for her. For an instant, she sought to pull away. Then an imp of mischief caught hold of her, and she pressed even more tightly against him and opened her lips. She had only meant to tease him. Instead, she felt herself caught up in a vortex of emotion unlike anything she had ever known. . . .

SIGNET Romances by Lynna Cooper

- [ ] **PORTRAIT OF LOVE** (#E9495—$1.75)*
- [ ] **HEARTS IN THE HIGHLANDS** (#E9314—$1.75)
- [ ] **FROM PARIS WITH LOVE** (#E9128—$1.75)*
- [ ] **SIGNET DOUBLE ROMANCE—HER HEART'S DESIRE and AN OFFER OF MARRIAGE** (#E9081—$1.75)*
- [ ] **FORGOTTEN LOVE** (#E8569—$1.75)
- [ ] **HER HEART'S DESIRE** (#W8454—$1.50)
- [ ] **MY TREASURE, MY LOVE** (#AE1668—$1.75)
- [ ] **AN OFFER OF MARRIAGE** (#AE1672—$1.75)
- [ ] **SUBSTITUTE BRIDE** (#AE1673—$1.75)
- [ ] **THE HIRED WIFE** (#AE1671—$1.75)
- [ ] **THE STARS CRY LOVE** (#AJ1427—$1.95)

*Price slightly higher in Canada

Buy them at your local bookstore or use this convenient coupon for ordering.

THE NEW AMERICAN LIBRARY, INC.,
P.O. Box 999, Bergenfield, New Jersey 07621

Please send me the books I have checked above. I am enclosing $_____
(please add $1.00 to this order to cover postage and handling). Send check or money order—no cash or C.O.D.'s. Prices and numbers are subject to change without notice.

Name_____

Address_____

City _____ State _____ Zip Code _____

Allow 4-6 weeks for delivery.
This offer is subject to withdrawal without notice.

Deep Water, Deep Love

BY
LYNNA COOPER

A SIGNET BOOK
NEW AMERICAN LIBRARY
TIMES MIRROR

PUBLISHER'S NOTE

This novel is a work of fiction. Names, characters, places, and incidents either are the product of the author's imagination or are used fictitiously, and any resemblance to actual persons, living or dead, events, or locales is entirely coincidental.

NAL BOOKS ARE AVAILABLE AT QUANTITY DISCOUNTS WHEN USED TO PROMOTE PRODUCTS OR SERVICES. FOR INFORMATION PLEASE WRITE TO PREMIUM MARKETING DIVISION, THE NEW AMERICAN LIBRARY, INC., 1633 BROADWAY, NEW YORK, NEW YORK 10019.

Copyright © 1982 by Lynna Cooper

All rights reserved

SIGNET TRADEMARK REG. U.S. PAT. OFF. AND FOREIGN COUNTRIES
REGISTERED TRADEMARK—MARCA REGISTRADA
HECHO EN CHICAGO, U.S.A.

SIGNET, SIGNET CLASSICS, MENTOR, PLUME, MERIDIAN AND NAL BOOKS are published by The New American Library, Inc., 1633 Broadway, New York, New York 10019

First Printing, August, 1982

1 2 3 4 5 6 7 8 9

PRINTED IN THE UNITED STATES OF AMERICA

One

SHE DID NOT see the shadow trailing her.

She swam swiftly, surely, deep beneath the surface of the ocean, her eyes watching the changing patterns just beneath her, where sea anemones swayed to invisible currents, where a fish darted from her path. Somewhere in these sands that spread far and wide beneath her was that one thing for which she searched: a hint of rotted wood or rusted metal. . . .

The shadow moved closer. As it did, some sixth sense alerted Kai Pierce. Her goggled head turned sideways and upward, and she saw the man with a knife in his hand, swimming strongly, right toward her.

Kai choked off a scream, kicked even more powerfully, aided by the Swimaster flippers on her feet. She shot upward, knowing her heart was hammering madly, wildly! That man was coming for her, to kill her. It was impossible to avoid him. He was too close! A single sweep of his arm would drive that length of sharp steel into her body.

To her amazement, nothing happened to her. She swam toward the surface, moving as fast as arms and flashing legs could take her. Yet that man would be behind her, seeking to bloody his knife in her flesh. She forgot everything in her desperate hurry, except swimming.

Kai popped to the surface, tore the air tube from her lips, breathing deeply of the fresh air, seeing the *Dolphin* where her brother stood.

Kai screamed.

Her brother came alive, jerking sharply and then leaning forward, hands on the gunwale. "What's wrong? What is it?" he yelled.

She did not bother to answer him. Instead, she began swimming toward the boat, swiftly, with the fear of death still pounding in her flesh. Her brother was at the *Dolphin*'s wheel, swinging the boat about, heading right at her.

In moments, he was leaning overside, a hand outstretched, catching her hand, lifting her up from the water, helping her over the side to stand dripping beside him. Concern was etched on his suntanned face, worry looked at her from his brown eyes.

"A man tried to—to k-kill me down there," she panted.

Amazement and disbelief were in the face that looked into hers. "Kill you? But why? What did you see? The treasure? Did you find the *Santa Maria Gloriosa?*"

Kai stamped her bare foot. Tears leaped into her eyes. She was close to hysteria. "No, I didn't find the *Santa Maria Gloriosa!* I didn't see a damned thing except sand and fish and weeds! But there was a man down there with a knife, and he was trying to kill me!"

He put his arms around her. "Hey, easy! You're safe now. Relax, will you? Nobody's going to kill you." He squeezed her harder. "See? You're fine. Just excited and scared, that's all."

"That's all?" she howled. "How would you have liked to be all alone down there with a madman coming for you with a knife in his hand?"

"Go dry off and put some warm clothes on. I'll start up the engine and we'll go back in. You've done enough for today. What you need is a good dinner and a long night's sleep."

She glared at him, pushed free. Trust a brother to think she was an hysterical female, filled with thoughts of murderers and hobgoblins! Ha! If he'd been down there instead of her, he wouldn't be so calm.

She was turning away when she saw the other boat, moving steadily across the waves toward a swimming man. Kai froze, scarcely breathing.

"There he is—the guy that tried to kill me!"

Ken Pierce swung about, staring. Then he relaxed, grinning. "Hey, that's the professor. That's his boat, the *Atlantis*. Rod Grant wouldn't hurt a fly."

She eyed her brother incredulously. "Not a fly, maybe. But a girl—yes! I tell you he tried to stab me with a knife." Kai stamped her foot. "Oh, why won't you believe me?"

"Because I know the guy. He's something else. Teaches underwater archaeology at the university. He's a member of the Institute of Nautical Archaeology. He's a very well-respected member of the community, Kai." Her brother grinned. "He's a woman hater, I know, but he doesn't carry his hates to such an extent as you seem to think."

Kai ignored him. What sense was there in talking to a brother who had his preconceived ideas? Her hands reached out for the powerful Fuginon binoculars resting on a hatch covering. Moving the lenses to her eyes, she stared hard.

She saw a man rising upward from the sea, a man with a heavy tan, with thick blond hair, muscles bunching in bulges all over his bare back as he clambered aboard the *Atlantis*. He stood a moment, shedding water, wearing a Jantzen swimsuit, sliding out of the straps that held his Swimaster aqualung. And—there was a belt about his middle, a belt that held a scabbard into which was thrust the knife she had last seen in his big right hand.

She lowered the binoculars. "I'm going to the police. I'm going to accuse him of attempted murder."

Her brother gripped her arm hard. "You're going to do no such thing. The police would only laugh at you. Rod's best friends with a police lieutenant who knows him as well as I know you."

Kai gaped at him. "I tell you it happened! He tried to kill me!"

"You made a mistake. I don't know what happened down there, but I know—as surely as I know we're standing here—that Rod Grant would never try to kill you." He chuckled suddenly. "If he had been trying to, you wouldn't be here now.

"Rod's the finest swimmer I ever saw. He's won medals for swimming. You couldn't have escaped from him, not if he really wanted to catch you."

Kai felt doubt touch her. If Rod Grant had wanted to kill her, why had he let her swim away? She was a good swimmer, but a man like this professor could have overtaken her very easily. He had been right above her, or almost, just about within touching distance. She scowled.

He tried to kill me. I know it. Nobody's going to make me change my mind!

Mutinously, she went on staring at his boat. It was turning, swinging about, moving toward the *Dolphin*. The big man with the thick thatch of pale gold hair was at the rail, looking at them. After a moment he waved.

"She all right?" he called.

"Fine, Rod. Just shook up, that's all."

"It was a near thing, down there. I'm glad she's safe, now."

Ha! Soft soap to try and make her ignore that fact that he was a homicidal maniac! Well, she wouldn't forget. Not her. She glared across the waves at this bronzed professor who didn't look at all like any professor Kai had ever seen. He resembled a Viking with that spread of muscular shoulders and that deep chest, that thatch of thick, golden hair. His middle was lean and ridged with more muscles.

Kai sneered. She had his number. He might fool everybody else, but he didn't fool her. He was a madman. She went on glowering, refusing to answer his friendly wave as the *Atlantis* turned westward.

She shivered suddenly as a breeze swept across the deck, chilling her damp flesh. She wasn't going to dive any more today. She might even be through with diving forever. Those depths down there were dangerous. She turned away, lips quivering, brushing at the tears that came into her eyes.

Moving into the cabin as Ken went to the wheel, she began to slide out of her swimsuit. As her eyes caught the mirror on the doorback, she paused to stare at herself. Rich brown hair hung down to her shoulders, and dark brown eyes peered out of a suntanned face. Ripe red lips seemed almost to pout at her above a dimpled chin.

She had never before thought of how she might look to a man. She had been a tomboy in her early childhood, right into her teens. Always, she had tagged after her brother Ken, playing ball with him, swimming, diving, steering the boats they had owned. Even in college, she had scorned the dates the other girls had doted on, studying all she could, knowing even then that what she had wanted to do was go after buried treasure, along with Ken.

Kai straightened and pushed at her hair, thrusting it back from her face. Was she pretty? Attractive to a man? A faint flush touched her cheeks, barely visible through her tan. Why should she care how she looked? There was no man in her life.

And yet. . . .

She could see Rod Grant standing in that boat, massively muscled and lean. His face was handsome in a rugged sort of way, under that shock of yellow hair. He looked primordial, somehow, very masculine. Kai supposed his girl students fell for him in droves.

Ha! Did he fall for them? Did he have a new conquest every term? Some simpering student who gave him her body in exchange for good marks? It would be just like him. Maybe he really hated women. Maybe that was why he had sought to kill her down there in the ocean depths. Yes, that must be it. He hated women, and he had seen a good chance to hurt one of them, unseen.

She pulled on a dirty sweatshirt and then slid into even dirtier dungarees that had oil spots and grease smears on them. What did she care how she looked? There was only her brother to see her.

Kai went topside and sat on the stern cushions as the *Dolphin* chugged along toward port. Her eyes scanned the sea before her, saw the *Atlantis* as a mere dot, far ahead. At least he owns a good boat, she told herself. No wonder. If he went about killing females under the sea, he needed to be able to make a fast getaway!

Suddenly, she felt miserable.

"Hey, take the wheel," her brother called.

She rose and moved forward, gripping the wheel, feeding more gas to the motor. She wanted to be off the waves and in the house for a nice warm bath. She needed to wash away all memory of this afternoon from her mind as she soaped away dirt from her body.

Kai used the *Atlantis* as a beacon, following in her wake. Oooooh! Would she like to come face to face with Roderick Grant! She would claw his eyes out! And slap that sun-bronzed face of his! Scowling, letting her thoughts run riot, she came after the boat ahead of her like an avenging fury.

He was still on the *Atlantis,* Kai saw as she maneuvered the *Dolphin* in against the quay. She drew a deep breath. It was now or never. He was stepping onto the quay, beginning his walk toward the land.

Kai lashed the wheel and all but ran to the gunwale, stepping up onto the wooden plankings. Behind her, she heard Ken say something, but she paid no attention. All her senses were concentrated on overtaking the big man ahead of her.

She ran, calling out, "Hey, you. I want a word with you!"

Rod turned just as her toe hit a plank that was somewhat warped and jutted upward above the others. Kai pitched forward, off balance. She was going to hit those planks and land on her front, right before this man she hated so much!

And then. . . .

Powerful hands caught her, lifted her upward as though she weighed nothing. Those hands raised her up off the quay so that she hung suspended in midair. Intensely blue eyes laughed down at her.

"Well, hello. You're an impetuous little thing, aren't you?"

Her tongue was frozen in her mouth. She could not

speak. All she could do was hang there in midair. We-ell, she wasn't entirely in midair, either. For he had used his big hands to bring her in closer, so that she found herself pressed up against his body. She could feel his muscles, now. They seemed to be all over the place.

And those arms of his had shifted position, to wrap themselves around her, clamping her right up against him. For a brief moment, it seemed he meant to crush her to death.

"You almost k-killed me," she whispered.

What was wrong with her voice? She just couldn't seem to talk properly. What was *wrong* with her? Why was she lying against this man and letting him do whatever he wanted with her?

"I'm sorry to have scared you," he said softly. He had such a deep, resonant voice! It went right through her. "But I was late. For that, I apologize, very deeply."

What was the big goon talking about?

Her mind was reeling, she just couldn't think, not with her softness being pressed so firmly against his hardness.

He kissed the tip of her nose.

Kai opened her mouth to yell, but her brother was saying, "I'm glad you two have met. Rod, this is my silly sister, Kai. That's K-a-i. Her real name is Catherine, but she likes the fancy spelling. Kai, this is Rod Grant. I hope you two become good friends."

There was a pause, then Ken said, "For goodness sake, Kai. Stop shoving yourself at the man, will you?"

"She almost fell, Ken. I had to grab her to prevent her from hurting herself. These quay boards are old and dry. She might have run splinters into her hands."

The arms were relaxing, easing her sneakered feet down onto the planks. Kai almost staggered when he let her go, but the hands came back to catch her, hold her. Those deep blue eyes were laughing at her again.

"Take care of yourself, now," he was saying, then turning and moving away.

Ken asked, "Why'd you throw yourself into his arms? I thought you didn't like him."

She had never felt more like screaming. She wanted to lift up her face and howl at the sky. The utter injustice of it all! Kai eased some of the fury in her by stamping at the quay with both feet, in a crazy dance.

"I did *not* throw myself into his arms! I started to fall and he caught me! He is the biggest, most pompous fool I have ever encountered! Worse than that, he's a born killer. A would-be murderer! And he *kissed* me. Do you hear that? He kissed the tip of my nose!"

Ken was laughing, leaning against the side of a piling, bent over and holding his stomach with both arms. Kai regarded him haughtily, eyebrows arched.

"You can see humor in this? Your sister is assaulted—this time, before your very eyes!—and you can do nothing more than lean there and laugh like the big jackass you are?"

"I never thought I'd see the day," he managed to gasp.

"Day? What day?"

"The day you finally fell in love."

Kai went rigid. "Have you gone insane? Has all the world gone nuts? Love that maniacal monster? I hate him. I hate his face. I hate his hair. I hate those blue eyes of his! I hate him all over!"

Ken was still helpless with laughter. Furious, Kai sniffed, turned her back, and marched away. She was so angry, she shook. Her brother was an idiot, an utter moron. She had always supposed him to be very level-headed, with both feet planted firmly on the ground. But to accuse her of having fallen in love! And with that homicidal maniac!

She moved to their somewhat battered old Ford. As she did so, she saw a sleek yellow Continental slide past. The man behind the wheel was Roderick Grant. Kai came close to gibbering.

She opened the Ford door, got in, and slammed the door. Almost at the same moment, Ken joined her, his face still creased with a grin, his eyes dancing.

"You could do worse," he said as he started the motor.

They drove in silence for a few minutes, then Kai murmured icily, "I hope you are not referring to what it is I think you're referring to."

"Sure I am. Rod. He's some catch, believe me. He has money he hardly knows about. He lives very simply.

Banks all his paychecks, his dividends, his royalties. Man's a hermit. Needs a loving wife."

Kai gritted her teeth. "I would be dead within a week."

Ken shook his head. "The man's a pussycat, for all his size. He'd be a pushover for someone like you, a real go-getter."

"The man's a born killer."

"It wasn't Rod down there who tried to knife you. Someone else. I'll bet on it. He drove off that other guy. You wait, you'll see."

Kai sneered. "I know what I saw."

"So what did you see? You saw Rod with a knife in his hand, apparently coming toward you. Couldn't he have been swimming toward whoever it was that was really out to get you?"

Kai told herself to keep calm. "Is there any reason you know why someone would want me dead?"

"We-ell, no."

"There! You see?"

Ken shook his head in that slow, irritating—to Kai—way he had. "There's no reason we know, or can think of, at the moment. But I'll bet you there is a reason."

She turned and stared at him. "Have you gone off your rocker?"

Her brother growled stubbornly, "Only crazy people try to kill others without a reason. *Somebody* tried to do you in. I have a hunch I know the way to find out."

"How?"

Ken grinned at her. "I'll tell you when I get around to it."

Kai gritted her teeth. She hated it when her brother got secretive like this. She knew well enough that she could never cajole him into telling her, once his mind was set against it. The best thing to do was forget about it.

Instead of pulling into the driveway of their little house, Ken stopped at the curb. When Kai glanced at him inquiringly, he said, "Got to go see somebody. Be back in an hour or so."

His eyes ran over her. "Put some decent clothes on, will you? All you ever wear are those jeans and that dirty sweatshirt. Try being a little feminine."

Her jaw dropped and she stared after him as the car pulled away. It wasn't like Ken to criticize her, either her clothes or her conduct. What was in his mind? She sniffed and moved toward the house. She was *not* going to change, she was *not* going to put on different clothing. Why should she? Just to cook some steak and onions and potatoes for dinner?

It was close to an hour and a half when her brother returned. Kai was scrunched up in a chair studying a map when he came in, grinning from ear to ear.

"Let's go," he yelled. "We're going out to dinner." He came to a stop and surveyed her. "Will you go put something clean on?"

"I'm happy as I am, thank you. And I do not intend to go out for dinner."

"Lobster with all the trimmings at The Wharf."

Kai glanced up from her study of the underwater currents around Sands Key, suspicion in her faint frown. "How come lobster in the middle of the week? How come lobster at all, now that I come to think of it?"

"We've been invited out."

"By whom?"

"It's a surprise. Now will you stop asking questions and go put on a dress?"

Kai shifted her position, folding the map. "Not until I learn who it is who's playing good fairy."

"Suit yourself."

Ken walked away, and there was something about the manner of his walk that intrigued her. Ken knew something, something in which he took secret delight. Oh, she knew him well enough for that. She pondered, sitting there, balancing her laziness against the thoughts of a three-pound lobster and melted butter. The lobster won.

Kai walked toward her room, calling out, "Okay, okay. You win. I'll go make myself gorgeous."

She opened her closet door, and made a face. She didn't have too many nice clothes; she had never cared much about her appearance, especially now that she was engaged in treasure hunting. Fancy clothes could come later, after she and Ken had found the remains of the

Santa Maria Gloriosa and the jewels and gold bars it had held when it had gone down.

There was her Sunday-go-to-meeting dress, of course, the Enka casual in burgundy which she had splurged on a year or more ago. By rights, she ought to wear that. But an imp inside her made her pass it over to check on whatever else she might have here that looked reasonably decent. Ah, yes. This A-line, rib-knit skirt by Ami ought to do, along with the Bago bubble-stitch striped sweater. After all, The Wharf wasn't the Waldorf.

She saw disapproval in her brother's eyes as soon as he saw her.

"You could have worn something a little classier," he muttered.

He himself was in a cotton corduroy sports jacket by Ralph Lauren, together with Halrin slacks. He looked quite the dashing young man about town, she thought morosely, and was tempted to go back and put on the Enka creation.

Oh, forget it. She was clothed well enough. Kai snatched up her worn handbag, eying its scuffed sides, noting a stain or two that she had always ignored. Who were they dining with, anyhow? Pierre Cardin? Setting her jaw firmly, she trailed Ken out to the Ford.

The Wharf was busier than usual, she noted as they pulled into the parking lot. Trust the summer visitors to know where to come to get good food! Ordinarily, there was no problem about parking, but Ken had to circle the area twice before he found an empty space.

As soon as they entered, the maitre d' was beside them, smiling and bobbing his head, gesturing for them to follow. Kai glanced at her brother, eyebrows arched. In the past, that same maitre d' had always ignored them, leaving them to find their own table. Now, however, they seemed to be people of importance.

The maitre d' even held her chair, bowing and smiling. When he had gone, Kai leaned forward over the table. "Who are we dining with, the King of Florida?"

Ken merely smiled and shook his head. "He'll be a little late, he's doing some shopping."

Kai raised her eyebrows. "Oh? Shopping for what?"

"Look at the menu, Sis."

"I don't have to. I know what I'm going to have. A three-pound lobster." She hesitated, then asked, "Are you certain we're his guests?"

Ken laughed. "Ask him. Here he comes now."

Kai raised her eyes and froze.

A man in a Skye tweed jacket—by Southwick, Kai knew—was moving toward them. His slacks were Halrins, and the foulard tie that fitted neatly with his Pierre Cardin shirt made him seem something that had just stepped out of a men's fashion magazine. Only after a swift survey of his clothes did Kai take notice of his face.

At first she did not know him. His thick blond hair was combed, his jaw freshly shaven. But the intensely blue eyes were the same: amused, yet faintly worried. He looked right at her, and his eyes asked a question.

Kai froze. She was not going to sit here with this killer! Her brother might, if he wanted. She was about to push back her chair and rise when Roderick Grant made her a little bow.

"I must apologize for being late," he said softly, his eyes never leaving hers. "It isn't easy to buy—what I had to buy. At least, for me it wasn't."

Curiosity made her sit down again. "And what is this mysterious something you had to buy?" she asked coldly.

Rod pulled back a chair, seating himself to Kai's left. There was a faint fragrance about him that pleased her. Some after-shave, no doubt. All the time, he looked directly at her. Almost annoyingly so. Kai felt her heart pounding crazily.

"Clothes," he said softly. "Female garments."

"I understood you aren't married."

He smiled, and Kai told herself that he had a fascinating smile. It lighted up his face, making him seem almost boyish. "I'm not. It's just—well, you might say I'm doing it to save a life."

"For a killer, you have a strange way of going about things."

He looked pained, and Kai felt a stab of guilt. Almost angrily, she told herself that this man deserved all the insults she could heap on him. Now he was turning away from her, toward her brother.

"It's all set," he said. "Not to worry."

Ken nodded, smiling. "In that case, let's eat."

Kai ran her eyes from one man to the other. There was something funny going on here, between her brother and this maniac. She might as well stay to learn what it was. Besides, she was hungry, and that three-pound lobster made her mouth water.

She said, too sweetly, "I've decided I want lobster. A three-pounder. We who are about to die might as well get a good meal."

Ken moved irritably, saying, "I explained what happened, Kai!"

"Sure you did. You said there was a man trying to kill me this afternoon. We're eating with him, right now."

Roderick Grant sighed. "I don't suppose it will make you change your mind, but there *was* a man just above you with a knife in his hand, swimming right at you. I came in from the side, and frightened him off. That's why you didn't see him. He was above and behind you. You could only see me, when you turned your head."

"It makes a good story, but it isn't true."

"Believe me," he said softly.

There was the ring of truth in his voice, but Kai ignored it. She knew what she had seen. She eyed him a moment, challengingly. Then she said, "Prove it."

"That's why we're here, among other things. You're in danger and your brother and I mean to see that you stay alive. And safe."

"This is ridiculous! There's no reason in the world why anyone would want to kill me!"

"No reason that we know."

Their eyes locked. His eyes were so gentle, so kind, so—so admiring!—that Kai felt as though she were another person. The strange thing was, she felt unable to tear her stare away. But she couldn't just sit here staring at him like this.

The waiter came, then, and they gave their orders.

It was Ken who picked up the conversation when the waiter had gone. "Any luck in your own dives, Rod? It seems to me that Kai and I have a ninety to one chance of success compared to what you're out to find."

Rod chuckled. "It's a way of spending a summer vacation, before I go back to lecturing at the university. I admit, it's a fool's dream, but then, I never laid claim to being anything but."

Kai asked, "What is it you're looking for?"

Rod said softly, "Atlantis."

"Your boat? Have you lost it?"

"No, no. I mean the original Atlantis, the island empire Plato spoke about in his Timaeus and Critias. You must know the story of Atlantis, how it existed somewhere in the Atlantic Ocean about eleven thousand years ago and how it disappeared in a single day and a night, beneath the ocean forever."

Kai stared. "You *are* nuts," she declared.

"Probably," he laughed. "But it gives me something to do with my time; it lets me swim about on the ocean bottom, looking for ruins. It also got me there at the right time to save your life."

Two

"OR TO KILL me," Kai murmured.

Those blue eyes of his fastened on hers. In a quiet voice, he said, "Had I wanted to, I would have." He drew a deep breath, then went on, "You were below me. I was swimming right at the man above you, but had I intended to run a knife into you, you'd never have escaped."

Something about the way he spoke told Kai he was speaking the truth. At least, the truth as he saw it. She remembered Ken's saying that Rod Grant was a marvelous swimmer. She herself was a good swimmer, but certainly not a superspeedster.

Just the same, she felt she was right. He had tried to kill her; or wanted to, at any rate. Kai had to admit that sitting here with him, seeing his bronzed good looks, his pleasant blue eyes, he certainly didn't seem to be a killer. Still! One never knew about kooks.

As if to taunt him, she smiled sweetly, saying, "You really don't honestly believe that there was an Atlantis, do you?"

"Of course there was. I think that's been proven. How else do you explain the great similarity between civilizations in Mexico and those in Europe? In parts of Asia, too, for that matter.

"Take your deluge legends, for example. The one most of us is familiar with is in the Bible, where Noah built an ark and saved himself and his family, plus a lot of animals, from drowning. But other nations had legends of a great deluge. The Babylonians and the Chaldeans, for instance. India also has its own story of the deluge, as related in the Rig-Veda, also in the Mahabharata, as well as in others."

Rod shrugged. "It just doesn't seem sensible to me that these stories, which go back many thousands of years, are unrelated. There was a catastrophe, the Flood. It destroyed a great island empire, Atlantis. As Plato says, Atlantis perished in a day and a night. Remember, that's a volcanic area, the middle of the Atlantic Ocean.

"The island of Atlantis just blew up. Tremendous internal pressures relieved themselves under it, and Atlantis was in the way."

Kai said, "Myths. Just myths."

"Oh, sure. I don't deny that. But everybody thought Homer's tale of the fall of Troy was a myth, too, until Schliemann unearthed the Troy of the Iliad, and then Mycenae. Nobody believed that such a city as Pompeii existed either, until it was found under the volcanic lava that Vesuvius spewed out.

"The trouble with looking for Atlantis is, there's no place to dig. The ocean covers up whatever ruins that may still exist, down there along the ocean floor. But it's there. There are some remnants to be found. I hope to do it."

Kai stared at him. "You're a dreamer."

He looked at her, and once more Kai felt the impact of those blue eyes. Something deep inside her turned over, and her heart commenced slamming again. This only made her more irritable.

"I suppose you have more proofs?"

"Oh, thousands of them. For instance, they built pyramids in Mexico as well as in Egypt. Pan was worshipped as a nature god in Greece, and also in Mexico and Central America. The Aztecs mummified the bodies of their dead, just as the Egyptians did. On both sides of the ocean, people believed in an afterlife and in souls, and both Aztecs and Egyptians had a high order of priesthood."

Rod smiled. "I could go on and on with comparisons. There is even a similarity in much of the folklore on both sides of the Atlantic, and in India as well. Why, all your people of the so-called New World had legends saying that they came from the East—that is, from Atlantis. They had monuments showing bearded men in Central America. How did the Indians, who have no beards, know about men with beards?"

Kai scowled. "Didn't somebody find Atlantis in the Aegean Sea a few years back? An island called Santorini?"

Rod shook his head. "Those who claim that ignore what Plato said. He claimed Atlantis was beyond the Pillars of Hercules—now the Straits of Gibraltar—and that there was a vast continent on the other side of Atlantis. In other words, North and South America. Solon, from whom Plato got his information, learned of Atlantis from Egyptian priests, who told him that nine thousand years before Solon's time, Atlantis had been utterly destroyed. Santorini still exists. It has not been destroyed, as was Atlantis."

Kai muttered, "Aside from trying to kill me, you seem like an intelligent man. Why waste your time on something like Atlantis?"

Rod chuckled. "As I said before, it gives me something to do during the summer months. Keeps me fit, swimming around down there on the ocean floor." He added, his eyes twinkling, "I even meet pretty girls down there, sometimes."

She sniffed, but she felt a little stab of pleasure run through her. Not that it mattered to her what Roderick Grant thought of her. After all, what does a victim care if her killer thinks she's pretty? Just the same....

Ken said, "I'm for more coffee. How about you two?"

"Might as well," Kai said. "It makes listening to fairy tales more enjoyable."

Rod laughed. He had a nice laugh, she thought, pleasant and unaffected. She wondered if he was laughing when he had tried to run that knife into her this afternoon. Probably, inside himself.

"Talking about fairy tales," Rod chuckled. "How are you two doing on your quest for sunken treasure?"

"Not too great," Ken muttered. "Nary a trace of anything down there. At least, I didn't see anything."

Kai snapped, "Sunken treasure is no fairy tale! People have become rich by finding gold bars and such in sunken ships. I don't believe I've heard of anybody becoming a millionaire by hunting for Atlantis."

"You have a point there," Rod nodded. "But I'm not after money. I'm after knowledge."

Ken hooted. "He has you there, Kai."

She scowled. By rights, she ought to be furious with Roderick Grant, but the more she studied him, the more he spoke, the more she was impressed by his good looks, his calm confidence. Oddly enough, this only angered her all the more.

"What's the name of this ship you're hunting?" Rod asked.

"The *Santa Maria Gloriosa*. It was a treasure ship, part of a fleet that was sailing from Cartagena to Spain in 1587. A storm came up, a violent one, and the fleet was scattered. The *Santa Maria Gloriosa* was wrecked offshore somewhere around here."

"You sure about that?"

"Well, no," Kai admitted grudgingly. "You can't be exactly sure of something like that. The way the gale was blowing, how far along on its course the fleet was, all these are imponderables."

Roderick Grant shook his head slowly. "Seems to me my attempt to find Atlantis is a lot more corroborated than your quest for this *Gloriosa*. At least, I think I know where Atlantis was."

"If it ever existed!" Kai snapped.

"Oh, I'm convinced of that. But this ship, now. The winds could have blown it anywhere from what is now Daytona Beach to Key West."

"That's encouraging," Ken growled.

"Hey, half the fun is in the looking. Look at all the exercise you two are getting out of this. All the fresh air, the swimming."

Kai frowned. "We're not doing it for those things."

"The money, then," Rod nodded. "All right, even from that angle, it isn't too bad. Most of your expense is for keeping the ship fueled and in good shape. The profits to be made are fabulous. Millions of dollars. You'll both be rich."

She eyed him. "You won't make a penny, even if you discover something that will prove there was an Atlantis."

Rod laughed. "Fortunately, I don't need much money. I certainly have enough for my everyday needs and then some."

"Suppose you get married?"

Kai couldn't help it. Those words had just come out. She flushed and bit her lip, but Rod Grant was nodding seriously.

"I'm lucky there. Marriage has never appealed to me. Probably because most young ladies I might consider would feel that I'm no better than a beach bum, swimming around in the ocean to find Atlantis. But it's the sort of life I like, especially in the summer."

It was the type of living she herself, and her brother, also enjoyed. In a sense, Roderick Grant was one with them in this. It was too bad he was a kook, swimming about with a knife in his hand to shove into girls he found swimming alone at the bottom of the Atlantic.

"You ought to join us," Ken said. "Come looking for the *Santa Maria Gloriosa*. You'd get all the exercise you'd want. And if we did find that ship with its gold, you could get a third share."

Kai sat up straight. Invite this murderer to go swimming with them? Had Ken lost all his marbles? She would no more go swimming where he was than she'd jump into a pool full of water moccasins! She was opening her mouth to protest when Rod beat her to it.

"Thanks for the invitation, Ken—but no. I have my own searching to do. The summer isn't long enough for me. Here it is late June, and I've only made half a dozen dives. I really ought to go out and stay out there on the sea, diving day after day, from sunup to sundown. That's the only way I'll ever find anything."

Kai relaxed. "I think you're nuts, but I do hope you find something—if there's anything to find, that is."

Rod smiled at her. "That's one of the things I find so admirable in you, Kai."

She tensed. What was he getting at? She asked, "Oh? What's that?"

"You're so sensible, so down to earth. You never permit yourself any flights of fancy. It's a very admirable trait."

Kai squirmed, not sure whether or not she liked this backhanded compliment. "At least, I know there *was* a *Santa Maria Gloriosa!* Records prove that. You can never be absolutely positive there ever was an Atlantis."

He shrugged his powerful shoulders. "I'm convinced there was. That's all that concerns me." He hesitated, glancing at her. "It's like love, in a way. Everybody tells me there's such a thing, but I've never found it. Have you?"

"Oh, love! That's for teenagers and songwriters."

His eyes searched hers. "You've never been in love, I take it?"

"Of course not!"

"I don't know why that should please me so much, but it does."

"How I feel about love is none of your business!"

"Certainly not! I was just asking. A pretty girl like you—one would think you'd have to beat suitors away with a wooden paddle."

Kai sat up. "Are you making fun of me?"

Rod was contrite. "Making fun? I was admiring you. Or can't I even pay you the compliment of doing that?"

She felt at a loss. Never one to bandy words with any male, keeping much to herself—outside of being with her brother day after day for years—she found herself wishing for the quick quip, the clever saying that would absolutely demolish this man. Instead, she felt herself to be tongue-tied.

It was her brother—grinning from ear to ear!—who

said, "Kai feels that falling in love is like a mental aberration. To be pitied."

Rod nodded. "My own feeling, exactly." His eyes laughed as they swung toward Kai. "You see, we agree on something."

She reached for her purse. "It's getting late. I want to thank you for the dinner. It was divine. And I did enjoy our talk."

She did not see her brother glance at Rod, did not notice both men nod and smile a little. Instead, she fumbled in her handbag, taking a moment to stare at her reflection in the little mirror before lifting out a lipstick and applying its gloss to her mouth.

Rod was standing; he moved to draw back her chair. They let her precede them between the tables, and caught up with her at the door, which Rod held open.

It was a clear, moonlit night, rather warm and sultry. In the background, they could hear the splash of the waves against a piling and caught the scent of salt water in the air. Faintly, they could hear a woman singing.

"We'll walk Rod to his car," Ken said, catching his sister by the elbow.

She turned to stare at him in surprise. Her brother had never been so solicitous of anyone before, to her knowledge. It was on the tip of her tongue to disagree, intending to pull clear of his hand and walk to their Ford by herself.

Kai shrugged. It made no difference to her if they walked toward the big Continental. There they would say their farewells, and she would never see Roderick Grant again. Not if she could help it, that is.

Her eyes ran over his car. It was an expensive one, tinted a yellow that was almost gold, and highly polished. It must have cost him a small fortune. Kai sneered. A showoff, that's what he was. A showoff and a murderer. A man she would say good night to as pleasantly as she could make herself, and never see him again.

He was unlocking the door of the big car. Then he turned to Ken, gripping his hand and shaking it. He turned to her.

Kai was about to hold out her hand.

To her stunned amazement, Rod bent over, putting out his arms. Then he was lifting her off her feet and depositing her inside the car. He closed the door on her and locked it.

Kai was speechless. She looked through the window at her brother, as though expecting him to explode into action. Instead, he was grinning, waving a hand at her, turning away on a heel. She stared after him, absolutely paralyzed.

Then Rod was in the driver's seat, turning the key in the ignition, bringing the motor to life. Kai stared at him, her mouth open. Had the man gone crazy? Had her brother, too, gone mad?

Three

As THE CONTINENTAL slid out of the parking lot and along the street, Kai told herself to be calm. This was not happening. It was a dream. She had escaped death at the hands of this man just this afternoon. Now he was taking her off somewhere—with her brother's full cooperation!—to murder her in some secluded place.

Calmly, she said, "This is a joke of some sort. You and Ken expect me to get hysterical, don't you? I'll yell and scream and you'll both have a good laugh. You'll stop the car and let me out, and you'll both fall on the ground, laughing so hard."

"Not at all. You have it all wrong."

She eyed him carefully. Well, he didn't seem crazy. Nor did her brother, come to think of it. Just the same. . . .

"If you think I'm going to ride off with you somewhere, you're very much mistaken."

"It's for your own good."

"For my own good?" she repeated numbly.

"Somebody wants you dead. Ken and I don't know who it is, but we're getting you off somewhere so your would-be killer won't be able to find you."

Kai seethed, trying to find words to cut into the quiet calmness of this man. "You're the one who tried to kill me! I saw you! Now Ken's played into your hands. He's given me to you, to kill me any way you like!"

"Don't be an idiot!"

Kai screamed. She opened her mouth and let go with a yell that reverberated throughout the car. She clawed at the door handle before she realized that the door was locked and that the button that permitted it to open was beside the driver. She kicked her feet on the floor pad, then lifted her purse and drove it at his face.

Rod braked the car, ducking the purse. He managed to steer the car to the side of the road and then he turned to her. His hands went out, caught her arms by the wrists, and brought her arms back behind her. At the same time he used those arms to bring her up against him.

Then he kissed her.

The kiss was hard, hungry. Yet it was gentle, too. It was the first time in her life Kai had ever been kissed so breathlessly, so furiously. She was being held against his chest, unable to move. And she had been taken so much by surprise that, before she was aware of it, she was kissing him back.

Realization came to her. She fought, then, as much as she was able to, struggling fiercely, seeking to escape those powerful arms. "Let me go, let me go," she panted.

"When you realize I'm doing this to help you," he whispered against her mouth.

Kai was speechless.

"Little darling," he murmured, leaning to kiss her nose, her forehead. "Can't you understand that I'm here to help you stay alive? Can't you trust me? Can't you trust your brother?"

She relaxed a little and found herself held tightly, almost cuddled against his deep chest. She breathed fitfully, she knew her heart was pounding away crazily, and—we-ell, she had to admit it wasn't totally bad, being held this way and whispered to.

"You're a beautiful girl," his voice went on gently. "I don't want anything to happen to you. Understand that, please! I'm here to help you. I'd die myself before I let anything happen to you."

"You would?" she whispered in surprise.

"Very happily. I've never met anyone like you. If I didn't know myself better, I might almost think I've fallen in love with you."

She whispered, "You tried to kill me."

"No, I didn't. I saved your life. Someday I hope I can make you see that. Right now, of course, you're convinced that I'm a maniac, that it was you I was swimming toward. I don't know of any way to change your mind except by taking very good care of you for the next week or two."

"*Week* or two?"

"While Ken tries to discover what's behind all this."

Kai gave that some thought. She knew her brother, or thought she did. If Ken was working hand in glove with Rod to get her off somewhere, maybe—just maybe—there was a reason for it. But what reason could there be? Nobody wanted her dead. She hadn't done anything to anybody. She knew very few people around town.

She sighed. It was almost pleasant to be cuddled so, and held so masterfully. If only Rod were not the would-be killer she knew him to be, she could enjoy this, very much.

"Wh-where are you taking me?" she asked in a small voice.

"To my secret hideout."

She slid her eyes up to peer at him. He was smiling at her, and his eyes were almost tender. Then he shook his head, still holding her eyes with his.

"There's no use trying to wheedle it out of me. You'll learn, soon enough. Now. Are you going to be a good girl and sit quietly beside me?"

"I guess so," she mumbled. What else could she do?

He bent his head and kissed her lips again. It was a very gentle kiss, and Kai could not prevent the way it sent hot thrills all through her body. But that was just the physical response to the kiss, she assured herself. It meant absolutely nothing. Except, of course, if he got murderous again. Maybe kissing would soothe him until she could get away.

She sat back in the seat as he removed his arms and turned toward the wheel. She was very much aware that she had responded to his kisses, and felt anger because of it. Her eyes went out the side window. They were moving along Route 1. Where could he be taking her?

He was driving faster, now, swinging onto Route 80, that cut across the Everglades. Kai sat up straighter, peering out into the darkness. All around them was swampland, and she could catch glimpses of water, tinted silver by the moonlight. It was quiet here, almost eerily so. The thought touched her mind that Roderick Grant could kill her very easily out here, weight down her body and toss it into this watery wilderness.

She shivered, unconsciously moving closer to this quiet man who drove so easily. Her eyes touched his face, seeing it calm and purposeful. He really didn't seem the type who went around murdering girls. But then, what was that type?

They went along beside the Tamiani Canal, then Rod swung the car northwestward past Forty Mile Bend. Ochopee lay ahead of them, Kai knew, and beyond that, Naples on the west coast. Could that be where he was headed?

Then he was braking the car, pulling it over onto some grass, shutting off the motor. Kai shifted uneasily. Was this where he intended to murder her?

"We're here," he said with a smile.

"Where's here? It looks like the middle of nowhere."

"All the safer for you, Kai. I have a little cabin off there in the Everglades. You'll be perfectly safe there. Nobody will ever be able to find you."

She didn't know whether that was good or bad, but she watched him move around to her side of the car, and when he opened the door, she stepped out into utter quiet, into a night illumined only by the moon and by the stars that blazed down in all their glory. Somewhere off to one side, a fish jumped, making a tiny splash.

Rod went around behind the car to unlock the trunk. He lifted out a suitcase. At her stare, he chuckled. "I had to fetch some clothes for you. I hope they're all right. You can't wear that dress where we're going."

"Oh? And why not?"

"We're heading deep into the Everglades. You'll need old clothes there. Things to muck around in."

Kai eyed the suitcase suspiciously. "You picked out my clothes, did you?"

"Oh, they aren't very much. Just some things to cover you."

She closed her eyes. Not only was he going to murder her, he wasn't even going to let her be dressed decently when he did. The Lord alone knew what hideous garments he had brought along for her.

Kai watched as he carried the suitcase off to one side. To her surprise, she saw him step out onto some plankings. Intrigued, she trailed after him, discovering a pirogue tied by a rope to one of the pilings. Rod was stepping down into the boat, placing the suitcase under a thwart. Then he turned to her, holding out his hand.

"I can get in by myself," she told him.

She stepped forward quite confidently. Unfortunately, one of her high heels wedged itself into a crack. She stumbled, but righted herself, seeing Rod about to spring forward to catch her.

"I don't always fall down when I'm on a pier," she snapped, and took another step, after freeing her shoe. It was then that the heel broke off, unbalancing her.

She pitched forward, right into his arms.

Once again, she was caught and held, brought in against his body so that she grew aware of its hardness, even as he must have been made aware of the softness of her own flesh. His arms closed about her and he held her crushed against him.

"This is fun," he grinned.

"Let me go! This instant!"

"Did you do it deliberately? Tell me the truth! Did you?"

"I did not! And don't you dare kiss me!"

He did, of course. She supposed it was like a challenge to him. His kiss was firm, yet soft, and in it, Kai sensed the hunger in the man, the need he had for her. For an instant, she sought to pull away, then an imp of mischief caught hold of her, and she pressed even more tightly against him and opened her lips.

She had meant to tease him, then to rebuff him.

Instead, she felt herself caught up in a vortex of emotion unlike anything she had ever known. Indeed, she had always felt herself incapable of this furious hunger, this need for caresses, for affection. Always, she had been cold, very stand-offish.

But now!

Kai never knew how long their embrace continued. When it ended, her arms were about his neck, his hands were gripping her buttocks so tightly she was positive there would be black and blue marks on her. Yet she had reveled in this! She had enjoyed it!

Slowly, he let her go. As slowly, she drew away, not daring to look at him. What must he think of her?

"I—I didn't mean to. . . ." she began.

"I know who you are now," he said gently.

"Wha- what are you t-talking about?"

"You're an angel sent from heaven. You aren't a real live girl at all! You're made of dreams and golden fluff, of diamond-studded cobwebs! I'm going to wake up in a minute and find you gone."

"I'm real enough. I'll bet you've put black and blue marks on me, too—where you grabbed me."

He kissed the tip of her nose. "I'll kiss it and make it better."

"You will *not!!!*"

"We-ell, maybe not now, not here. But one day I will."

"You'd better not. I don't believe in love, nor in any of this silly, gooey stuff."

"Of course you don't. Neither do I."

He had not released the pressure of his arms, Kai noted. She also noticed that she was not struggling to get away. Now why was that? She was no giggling minx to play with a man's affections. For one thing, she didn't know how. Yet she was thoroughly content to lie against him like this, whispering nonsense.

"You don't?" she asked in a small voice.

"No more than you do."

"Well, I'm glad that's settled."

He let her go slowly, freeing her. Kai felt a little dizzy; she wasn't at all sure of her footing in this pirogue, especially after what had happened. But his hand was holding hers, he was guiding her, helping her to sit down on a thwart. Then he was turning away, to untie the rope that held the boat to the piling.

Rod lifted a long pole and dug it into the water.

Slowly, the pirogue moved forward.

It was so quiet here, even the gurgle of water about the prow seemed loud. All nature appeared to be hushed, asleep. Yet Kai knew there was life all around her. Alligators and turtles, crayfish and snails abounded here. Catfish and garfish, bullfrogs and lizards called these Everglades home. Up ahead there was a plop as a fish played, and off to one side, a frog croaked.

She glanced at Rod, standing in the pirogue, poling steadily. He was dressed as he had been, of course, yet even so, he did not seem out of place. It was almost as though he were on his way home. These Everglades were a part of him. She found herself wondering about the sort of man he was, who would be content to bury himself out here, deep in these swampy lands. It wasn't as if he were ugly or misshapen.

Looking at him, Kai had to admit that he was rather handsome, and his body was lean and muscular. Any girl would give her eyeteeth to latch onto him. Ken had told her a little about him, how he banked all his paychecks and lived on practically nothing, though he had a more than sizeable income from stocks and bonds in which he had invested.

Why, then, was he so much a misogynist? He didn't seem to hate women. Then why hadn't some girl latched onto him? Ha! Maybe he tried to murder any of them who so much as looked at him!

Almost against her will, Kai found herself smiling. He certainly hadn't treated her as might a man who hated females. On the contrary! He always appeared to be hugging and kissing her. Holding her much too close! She scowled. He would have to stop that if she were going to spend a week or so out here in these wilds with him!

And that was another thing. Why did he have to bring her way out here? Wouldn't she be just as safe in some apartment, closer to civilization? She shivered. He could do whatever he liked with her, off here where there was nobody around to stop him. She would have to be on her guard all the time.

They were moving steadily between the reeds and grasses, along a watery route he appeared to know very well. As much as she stared around her, no matter how she shifted on her seat, she could see nothing but sky and sawgrass. It was more than lonely here. It was desolate.

"Over there," he said at last, nodding with his head.

Kai squirmed about, saw a little island in the distance with a cabin rising upward. It was dark, that cabin, and looked almost gloomy. Is this where she was going to have to stay for all that time? She would go nuts!

"Do you bring all your girls out here?" she asked.

Now whatever made her say that? The words had just leaped from her tongue. First of all, she wasn't his girl. That was the most important fact. And she didn't want him to think of her in that way.

His chuckle was soft. "You're the first. As I already told you, I like my privacy. I'm only letting you come here because you're in danger. Ken has been here, of course. We've fished a lot, he and I, when he could tear himself away from his treasure hunting."

Mmmmm. Now that he mentioned it, she did recall that Ken had gone off by himself from time to time, taking his fishing tackle with him. So this was where he had come.

The pirogue ran up onto solid ground. Rod poled the boat firmly forward, anchoring it. Then he stepped forward, holding out his hand to assist her to rise. He guided her forward onto a bare patch of dirt. He turned then, lifting the prow of the pirogue, dragging the boat upward. Reaching into it, he caught up the suitcase and, with it in a hand, he walked ahead of her toward the cabin.

When he unlocked the door and lighted a lamp, Kai found herself looking around her at the neat interior. There were Indian rugs on the floor, and what appeared to be handhewn furniture—several chairs and a large couch. There was a kitchen and two closed doors that obviously led into bedrooms.

Rod closed the door and smiled at her. "Here we are, safe and sound. You're to take the room on the right. The other is mine. I'll carry your bag in for you."

Kai tossed her handbag on the handhewn table, noting that the tabletop was covered with books and magazines. Apparently, Roderick Grant did a lot of studying here. Well, it was a perfect place for it, being so isolated, so quiet. She moved toward the kitchen, wondering what sort of cook he might be. If he cooked anything, that is. Maybe he only bought frozen foods, and stored them in the big refrigerator. Faintly, she could hear the humming of a generator.

Rod came toward her as she was opening the fridge. "Care for a cup of coffee? I usually take some hot chocolate at this time. How about it?"

"Love some. No, no food. I was just nosey, poking into the fridge to see how well you ate here."

He grinned. "I don't skimp. I'm a good cook. I treat myself well while I'm here. Steaks, chops, cuts of roast beef, turkey breasts, hams. You'll find them all."

"You don't look as though you eat all that much."

"I don't. Friends drop in, from time to time."

Her eyebrows arched. "Friends? Out *here?*"

"Seminoles, for the most part. They know me from long ago, when I was in college. Whenever they see lights on, or smoke coming from the chimney, or see the pirogue out there, they know I'm home."

Kai eyed him. "No girls, hey?"

Rod laughed. "What girl in her right mind would come out to this wilderness? No, no. No girls. Not until you, that is."

She watched him prepare the chocolate to be heated. He was precise in all his actions, he certainly knew his way around this kitchen. Eyeing him, Kai felt an almost irresistible urge to take the pan away from him, to prepare the cocoa herself.

Yet when he brought her cup to her, filled to its brim with the hot chocolate—it even had a marshmallow floating on it——she had to agree it was very pleasant to be waited on in this fashion.

"You're a strange man," she said as she sipped. "I really can't believe that you have no girl friends."

"Oh, I know some girls. One in particular." He chuckled. "She wants to marry me."

Kai felt herself freeze. "Does she?" she asked coolly.

Rod spread his hands. "She seems to think I'd make her a good husband," he informed her almost apologetically. "I've taken her out to dances, to night clubs, things like that. Why not? But Sandra wants something more than dates."

"Sandra," Kai said thoughtfully.

"Sandra Alberts. You must have heard of the Alberts family. They own half of Florida, it seems. Hotels, citrus groves, cotton plantations. You name it, they probably have a finger in it."

"A rich girl, then."

"Very rich. An only child."

"And you won't marry her?" Kai asked in amazement.

Rod frowned. "She doesn't like the things I do. She'd want me to give up looking for Atlantis, she'd want me to give up diving, give up my professorship. Just count her money and squire her over half the globe."

"Sounds like a cushy job, to me."

Rod laughed. "That's exactly what it would be. A job. I like my lifestyle, I enjoy my independence. Why should I give it up?"

"Money is not to be sneered at."

"I have all the money I need."

Kai lifted her cup, stared down at the remnants of the hot chocolate. "Does anyone ever have enough money?"

"That all depends on what you want money to do for you."

"It would make you independent."

"Not if I married Sandra. Oh, maybe I will, some day. I've thought it over, from time to time. I've even told her that I must keep my professorship, I must keep my boat and go on diving during the summers."

"Why doesn't she go with you? It ought to make for a perfect vacation, off somewhere on that boat of yours, with nothing to do but swim and dive and laze about in the sun."

Kai became aware that there was a yearning in her voice, as though some secret part of her was making itself heard for the first time. But why not? This was how she lived her life, diving for sunken ships, for treasure. Of course, she did it with her brother, not with a husband.

Always, until now, she had been satisfied with her life.
I'm still satisfied! I have the best life possible!
Ah, but. . . .
Sometimes, even with Ken, she felt lonely. Ignored as a woman. It was all very well to dive and swim about, to share her meals with her brother. Yet there was something—she didn't know just what—that was missing.

Rod was speaking, she realized with a start.

". . . never agree to that. She has to have fine clothes, go to a beauty parlor every other day, it seems. She's always dressed as though she just stepped out of a fashion show."

He smiled at her. "You, now. You're different. You don't mind wearing old things, getting grease on your face."

Suddenly, she wanted to scream. Is this how he saw her? As some sort of—grease monkey? Only as a tomboy? Couldn't he tell that she was just as feminine as any other girl? As feminine as this Sandra Alberts? But no. Of course not. He was a male animal, blind to such niceties.

It was of a piece with his hunt for Atlantis. Atlantis! What a lot of nonsense! But then, he was a professor. And professors walked around with their heads in the clouds.

She brooded at him, suddenly angry. "Maybe marrying her would do you good. Get you out of this fantasy life of yours. Make you give up that crazy notion of finding Atlantis."

"Hey, you know you sound just like Sandra when she gets miffed."

"Oh, do I? Let me tell you something, Roderick Grant. You're stuffy! You run after pipe dreams! You're so wrapped up in your crazy lifestyle that you can't see what's best for you."

His blue eyes twinkled at her. "You sound more and more the way Sandra does. But maybe all women are the same. I suppose it's only natural. There's some instinct in them that wants to get them married and have kids and live sensible, sane lives."

Kai stiffened. "I do not want to get married and have babies. I live a very sensible, sane life right now."

"Sure you do. Hunting for buried treasure."

Her lower lip began to tremble. Oh, God! Was she going to burst into tears? Wetness began oozing from her eyes. If she began weeping now in front of him, she would die!

"Easy, now," he said abruptly. "I didn't mean to...."

It was too late. Tears were leaking down her cheeks, and she saw him through a wet blur. Her lips were definitely quivering, and so was her chin. In moments, she was going to wail out loud.

Rod leaped to his feet, came around the table to her, lifting her to her feet and folding his arms about her. "I'm a big gawk. I ought to be shot, telling you something like that."

"I—I've been p-poor all m-my life and this i-is the o-only way I know of g-getting some mo-money...."

She was really crying now, shoulders shaking, the tears running faster and faster out of her eyes and down her cheeks. She sobbed, burrowing her face into his chest, aware that his arms were hugging her tightly, as though sheltering her from everything unpleasant.

"Of course it is. I admire you, I really do. You know what you want and you go after it. I think that's terrific."

"You d-do?"

"Certainly I do! It isn't every girl who'd go diving down to the ocean floor day after day, looking for sunken ships. You're brave, you know what you want, and you go after it."

Kai sniffled and he reached for his handkerchief. She wiped her eyes, her cheeks, then blew her nose. "I must look a sight," she mumbled.

"Not a sight," he smiled. "A vision."

"Ha! With my eyes red and my nose all swollen?"

"Pretty nose," Rod said, and kissed its tip.

Kai scowled up at him. "You say you don't have anything to do with girls, yet you seem to know all the right things to say and do."

"If I do, it's because you bring them out in me."

Despite all she had thought about this man, Kai realized suddenly that she was enjoying being held so tightly in his arms; yes, and even having her nose kissed by him. What was the matter with her? The man was a would-be murderer! She was like a lamb cuddling up to the hungry wolf.

She opened her mouth to say something of this—and yawned.

Instantly, she was horrified. Both hands came up to her mouth and her eyes grew big as she stared up at him.

"You're tired," he stated, easing the grip of those strong arms. "You ought to be in bed."

"I'm sorry. I really am!"

"I'm the one who's sorry. I've kept you up drinking cocoa and talking, while all the time you should be getting your beauty sleep."

She was not struggling to get free of those relaxing arms. Instead, she was almost nestling closer. Kai could not understand herself. Maybe she did need sleep. As it was, she did not seem responsible for her actions.

Rod walked with her to the door of her bedroom. "I've put out the pyjamas I bought for you on the bed. Just put them on and fall into bed. I'll see you in the morning."

She closed the door, staring about the room. He had turned on a little bed table lamp, too. Its roseate glow showed her the maple bed, the matching bureau, a comfortable chair. It was a small room, but very neat. There were a couple of Frederick Remington prints on the wall, nicely framed.

Kai started to get undressed.

Morning sunlight woke her. She lay a moment, snuggling deeper under the sheet and blanket, still only half awake, half of her back in that dream she had been enjoying. In it, she and Rod had been swimming deeper and deeper in the ocean.

They had swum so far down that everything was dark about them, and then there had been light, and in that light she had seen an underwater castle, all glittery with gold and jewels. Its door had been open and Rod was swimming toward it. She tried to join him, to enter that fairy castle, but something had pushed her back, no matter how hard she tried to get to it.

Rod had turned back to her, then, holding out a hand, seemingly telling her that he would not go into that castle unless she went with him. She had wept, he had taken her in his arms and had kissed her. . . .

Waking, Kai wriggled protestingly. Why had the dream stopped just then? Why couldn't it have gone on just a little longer? Until she had been able to savor the delight of those kisses even more? It just wasn't fair.

Her eyes opened slowly. Sunlight was in the room, making it all golden, as though welcoming her to the new day. She turned onto her back and lay a moment, thinking.

She ought to be terrified, being here with Roderick Grant. The man had sought to kill her, and here she was mooning over him like an adolescent over some rock star. Very definitely, she was losing her grip. Where had the calm, composed Kai Pierce gone? A week ago, for anyone to have suggested she would be off here in the Everglades with a would-be killer—and to be enjoying the experience!—would have roused hoots of laughter in her.

Kai sighed and pushed back the covers. She might as well go and see what Rod was doing. Not until she was out of bed and reaching for the suitcase did it occur to her that she actually missed his presence.

"Nonsense," she snorted, and opened the bag.

She stared down at the clothes he had bought for her. She closed her eyes and looked again. This could not be. Had the guy gone nuts?

There was a blouse by Geoffrey Beene, a blouse by Ralph Lauren, short shorts by Sasson, loungers by Jordache, an ultra skimpy bra-and-panties swimsuit by Roxanne, lingerie, even Kimel pumps. . . .

Did he expect her to be a model in some sort of fashion show? All her life, she had worn jeans and sweaters:

cheap things that she didn't mind getting dirty, soiled by grease and oil. But these! It was almost as though he were trying to tell her something.

Kai scowled. Yes, that was it. He was trying to tell her that she was a slob, but he was trying to be subtle about it. In his eyes, she dressed like a lady bum. So! If he thought he was going to get away with that, he had a couple of thinks coming.

Her hands removed the pyjamas. Now that she came to think about it, those pyjamas were sheer silk, a creation by Shuba.

Angrily she slid into a sheer blouse, pulled up the short shorts. They showed an awful lot of her legs, and that blouse was pretty revealing, but she had to wear something. Scowling darkly, she turned toward the door—and caught sight of herself in the bureau mirror.

Kai gasped. Her eyes opened wide and for an instant she stood stock-still, staring. Was that she in that glass? That girl who looked so gorgeous, with her deep tan and all that thick brown hair, and those red, red lips? Her hair was tousled, true, but it added to her attractiveness in a hoydenish sort of way.

For almost the first time in her life, Kai thought of herself as a female. A female, that is, who would be attractive to a male. She turned slowly, eyeing her body. She could see quite a bit of it, she decided, realizing that what she was able to see, Rod would see, too.

Kai blushed. She could not go out like this, into the other room where Rod was probably waiting for her. She would be a walking invitation to rape. Her hands doubled up into fists. Just let him try. Just let him!

Frowning, she opened the bedroom door and marched into the kitchen. Rod was standing at the stove, looking down into a skillet. At the sound of her footsteps, he turned.

His eyes got big, his mouth fell open.

"Wow!" he exclaimed.

Something in his eyes kept her angry words frozen on her lips. She had never been looked at in this way: so worshippingly almost. It stopped her in her tracks.

"You're beautiful," he whispered.

Adoration was in his blue eyes. Quite slowly, he put down the spatula he had been holding and began walking around her, staring. Kai did not move. She could not. Every muscle in her body was paralyzed, except for her heart. That was slamming and banging away so wildly that she was positive he must hear it. It was hard for her to breathe, too.

"I knew you were pretty," he was saying. "I never realized how absolutely gorgeous you are. You're breathtakingly lovely."

"You're nuts," she breathed.

He came to a halt in front of her, staring down into her eyes with those blue eyes of his that had the power of reaching deep inside her. "No, I'm quite sane." He added with a grin, "At least, I think I'm sane. But being with you like this is a little disturbing. And I don't like being disturbed."

She frowned. "Disturbed?"

"I thought it would be a lead-pipe cinch to shelter you here in Everglades, alone with me for a week or two. Now, I'm not so sure."

"Oh? Why not?"

"I am human, you know. You're a walking temptation."

"Ignore me," she muttered.

"*Ignore* you? How, for Pete's sake? I can't tear my eyes away from you. I've never seen anyone like you. So beautiful. So exquisite."

All this time, Kai realized, they were staring at each other, just standing there, lost in the other's eyes. In a minute, he was going to step forward and take her in his arms. And kiss her. She knew it, just as she knew she was standing on the floor.

"You have to help me," he whispered.

"How? How can I help you?" she breathed.

"Go away. Go for a walk. Go back into your bedroom. Get out of my sight."

"Why should I do that?"

"Because if you don't, I won't be responsible for what might happen. I didn't bring you here to make love to you. I brought you here to protect you." He made a wry face. "You have to be protected, all right. But from me."

"I've known that all along. You're a murderer."

"Do you really believe that, Kai? Do you honestly think I could harm one hair of your gorgeous head?"

"We-ell, maybe not."

They couldn't go on standing here like this, just lost in each other, Kai told herself. There was food cooking on the stove. It would burn if it wasn't attended to. Phooey! Let it burn. She could always eat. A moment like this was too precious to end just because she was hungry.

Rod shook himself. "I'm a bad host. You must be starving."

She smiled up at him. "I could eat a little, I guess."

Kai sighed. If he wasn't going to grab and kiss her, there was no sense in standing here any longer. She would have to make the first move, she could see he certainly wasn't going to.

"What's for breakfast?" she asked.

"Bacon and eggs, toast and coffee."

"Won't the eggs burn?"

Ha! That did it. He started and then whirled back toward the stove. Kai sneered. Just like a professor. Always has both feet on the ground, never gets rattled enough to waste a couple of eggs. With his head in the clouds, too. Never kissing a girl when that's the one thing he should do.

She sank onto a chair, watching as he scooped bacon onto a plate and then placed eggs beside it. He handed the plate to her, then poured out some milk for her.

"Coffee, now? Or later?" he asked.

"Later."

"Good. That's when I have mine, after I've eaten."

She began to eat. Rod sat across from her, staring at her as though she was a magnet and his eyes were iron filings. It came to her that she was reveling in this adoration. Nobody had ever acted this way toward her, in her entire lifetime. She wanted it to go on and on. Still!

"Eat," she told him.

That seemed to break the spell. Rod gave his attention to his plate, eating like a man in a daze. The eggs and

39

bacon were very good, Kai decided. He might have his head in the clouds, but he knew his way around a stove. They were as good as she might make, and she prided herself on her cooking abilities.

Over coffee, she asked, "What do we do today? Or do we just sit around?"

"I'd planned on doing some fishing. If that's all right with you?"

"Great. I'd like that."

He eyed her dubiously. "Do you know how to fish?"

Kai gritted her teeth. "I'll have you know I've fished since I was no bigger than a kitten! Have you an extra pole and line?"

"Keep them for my guests. Any time you're ready, just say the word."

Carrying two poles, they went out into the morning sunlight. It was peaceful here, very quiet. Pausing to breathe in the clear, clean air, Kai began to understand the hold this cabin and its location might have on a man like Roderick Grant. It was like a little slice of heaven.

He poled the pirogue out into clear water. Kai stared at red mangrove trees, along with some buttonwood. Water shield pads at the edge of a marsh lay like strange green mouths, upturned to the heavens as though awaiting rain. In the background, she saw a wide stretch of marsh grass, bright green against the darker green of oaks wrapped about by resurrection fern. It was a wild place, this deep into the Everglades, a world all its own.

Rod placed the poles in the boat, reached for the fishing lines.

"We'll try for some large-mouth bass. I've found them in these waters before. Besides, they make good eating."

She watched his deft fingers attach bait—he must have dug up that bait earlier this morning—to the hooks. He was a strange man, this professor, to her way of thinking. True, she had few acquaintances by which to judge him, yet all the men she had known would have abhorred his way of life. Always by himself, content to be that way, seeming to have no need of others.

She wondered if he had ever fallen deeply in love and been jilted. Much to her surprise, she felt a sudden stab of jealousy. Oh, he was handsome enough, in his rugged way; considerate, too, and certainly polite enough. What was it about him that had kept him free of female pursuers?

Hmmmm. There was this Sandra Alberts person. From what he had said, Sandra wanted him to marry her. She could easily understand that. She guessed he was quite a catch for a woman. Unless other girls he had gone out with had recognized that need to kill in him. Could that be?

He handed her a pole. Kai took it, dropped the bait overside, and let out her line. But her mind was not on fishing. He didn't look like a murderer, but then, a murderer probably looked just like anybody else.

True, he had shown no disposition to catch hold of her and throttle her. Anything but! She scowled, recalling the times he had taken her in his arms and how she had enjoyed being held and fussed over. And that was strange, too. Never before had she liked anything like that. On the contrary, she had always avoided men, for that very reason.

Roderick Grant was a mystery. If she were a different sort of person, she would probably be after him, to learn what it was that made him the way he was.

He was sitting quietly, half turned away from her as though he had forgotten her existence, completely wrapped up in his pole, his line, and the bait that dangled down there in the water. Kai frowned. Now why should that bother her? He was nothing to her, she was nothing to him. Yet the sight of his broad back and lean middle annoyed her, for some obscure reason.

Something jerked her line. Instantly, she was awake, roused out of her thoughts, jerking up the pole so as to fix the hook more firmly in the fish's mouth. She was a little surprised at the force of the tug, and let the line out more, though keeping it taut.

She reeled in, let a little line out, reeled in again, keeping the pole high and bent. Kai forgot everything but the struggle, enjoying these moments of capture and combat. She played the fish carefully, firmly.

When it was at the side of the pirogue, she grew aware

that Rod was standing, the net in his hand. He dipped it into the water gently, then slid it sideways to scoop up the fish.

It was a big bass, she saw as he brought it into the air, wriggling and still fighting. Rod upended it into the bottom of the boat.

"You did that well," he said, with admiration in his voice.

"I've fished a lot with Ken. I'm no beginner."

"No, indeed. Too bad I didn't know a long time ago how expert you are. I'd have asked Ken to bring you here."

"I wouldn't have come."

He sat down on a thwart, still eying her. "Why not?"

"He leads his life, I lead mine. Except when we go diving, that is. I like it that way."

"Oh. You have boy friends who keep you busy."

Was that a touch of jealousy in his voice? Kai shook her head. "No. I have no men friends. I like to keep to myself."

He grinned at her. "Like me."

She looked at him hard. "You have a girl friend. That Sandra person."

"She's just a girl I know."

"Whom you're going to marry."

"I never said that. She wants to marry me, yes. But there's never been anything definite about it."

"Are you afraid of marriage?"

He smiled wryly. "Maybe I am. I've never thought too much about it, I've always managed to keep too busy for romance."

"Or were you just running away?"

Rod shook his head. "I don't think so." He frowned. "Or maybe I was. I'm not sure." His hand gestured at the loneliness about them, at the water and the distant grasses. "I like this sort of life. How many girls would? I like diving in the ocean, hunting for something that would make me certain I had found some remnant of Atlantis."

"There you go again. Atlantis! I'm surprised that a man of your educational background would believe in such a fairy tale."

"It has to be, Kai. There are too many similarities between the civilization of the Mayas, the Incas, and the Aztecs with those of Egypt and Phoenicia to admit of anything else. There has to be a connecting link between them. Even the Mahabharata of India speaks of the island in the Atlantic, and that it was destroyed in a great cataclysm.

"Something fell out of the sky. A huge meteor? A small moon? Who knows? But something fell, and landed on Atlantis. Atlantis was in a volcanic belt. That falling something broke open the earth's crust, or damaged it. The resultant volcanic explosion would have made the Krakatoa explosion seem like a mild breeze."

He shook his head. "There are too many hints. It had to be."

"You're really gung-ho about all this, aren't you?"

Rod laughed wryly. "I suppose I am. But the day is too nice to spend arguing. Here, give me your hook. I'll bait it again."

Kai fished, but her mind was not on it. What made a man like Roderick Grant tick? He was a romantic. Oh, sure. Only a romantic would set himself the task of trying to prove an Atlantis really existed. On the other hand, a romantic ought to be more concerned with girls. He was a strange contradiction.

Kai sighed. It made no never mind to her, of course. She couldn't care less about Rod Grant and any women he might know. Hmmm. If this were so, then why was she thinking so much about him?

She glanced at him. He was intent on his fishing, as usual. You would never know, by looking at him, that she was in the boat. Something stirred to life inside her. Maybe it was just her pride, but she did not relish being ignored in this way. Kai moved restlessly.

Still! Maybe it was a good thing he ignored her. Otherwise, she would have to be fighting him off all the time.

She began to dream. It was fun, being grabbed and held by him. Even kissed. She was honest enough to admit that. It was something entirely new to her. New—and sobering. How did she really feel about Roderick Grant?

Oh, she guessed she liked him, all right. He was her brother's friend.

"The net," he called.

She had known other men who were friends of her brother. None of them had ever appealed to her. With one or two of them she had had to come right out and let them know how she felt. She did not want to become emotionally entangled with any man. Not then, not now, not ever.

"Hey, the net!" he yelled.

Then why was she puzzling so much over this man? He had tried to kill her, she ought to hate him, to be afraid of him. She was not afraid, she was even having a good time, being out on the Everglades waters with him, fishing.

"Hey!" he bellowed.

Kai jerked free of her thoughts. "Wha-what is it?"

He was standing in the boat, his rod bent double, alternately reeling in and letting out line. And he was glaring at her.

"The net. I have a big one!"

She snapped to awareness, reaching for the net. He was maneuvering the fish in close to the boat, playing it nicely. Kai could see it now, a huge bass.

Gripping the net, she leaned over the gunwale, sliding the net into the water. Rod was swinging his pole around, bringing the bass within reach. Deftly she slid the net forward through the water, scooping up the fish.

It was a big one, all right. A six-or seven-pounder, at least. Rod was grinning from ear to ear, looking down at it flopping around on the pirogue's bottom. Kai watched him, thinking how much like a little boy he was, delighted with his catch.

"Had enough?" he asked. "We have our dinner, that's for sure. What say we call it a day?"

Kai shrugged. "All right with me. But what's to do once we get back to the cabin?"

Rod laughed. "You play cards? Or chess?"

She nodded slowly. "I play chess, yes. Ken taught me. I play with him, a lot."

"Do you? Hey, that's great. We'll have lunch, then I'll

get out the board and chessmen. We'll have a couple of games."

He reached for the pole, dug it into the water, and sent the pirogue moving forward. Kai sat swaying to the rhythmic surge of the boat, realizing that she was hungry, that being out in the open air was giving her an appetite. She frowned. This would never do. She had eaten a good breakfast, by rights she ought to skip lunch. But she would never be able to abstain from a sandwich and watch Rod wolf one down.

She stiffened, remembering the old adage about the condemned person eating a good meal. Was that what Rod meant to do? Stuff her full of food, then kill her?

Four

KAI CARRIED THE fish to the cabin while Rod followed with the poles. She grew aware that he was talking to her, and turned her head to look at him.

". . . haven't had a good chess game in so long I've almost forgotten how to play. You'll probably whip me something fierce."

She would enjoy that. Oh, how she would! Humble him, make him realize that she was nobody to treat lightly. It might be a good idea for her to get hold of a knife, maybe one of the sharp kitchen knives, and carry it with her from now on. She had been too trusting.

Now why was that? Certainly she had known that he was a killer, yet she was blithely walking around without a weapon to protect herself, just as a little rabbit might be trotting along, unaware that it was being stalked by a hungry wolf. She would make certain she had something close by with which to defend herself, from now on.

Yet as she watched him scale the fish, slice them open, and prepare them for storage in the refrigerator, she told herself that this man was no killer of women. Oh, sure, he was big and strong, and she would have no chance against him if he reached for her throat with his hands. But if she had a knife in her belt, or close by, she could always run it into him and flee in the pirogue.

He turned and smiled at her. His blue eyes were alight with pleasure. "I'm enjoying this," he told her. "It's fun. It's good to have you here, Kai."

Rod shook his head. "At first, I was doubtful about it. Oh, I admit it. When Ken suggested that I take you off with me, it was on the tip of my tongue to refuse. I'm no hand with women. I felt that I'd be walking into a boring limbo where I had to sit around and hold your hand, to cheer you up, to bolster your courage. But it isn't like that at all."

She flared, "If I'm such a nuisance——"

He turned and caught her by her shoulders. Drat! The touch of his hands was turning her mushy. "Hey! Don't misunderstand me. I'm giving you a compliment. I think you're the best thing that ever happened to me."

Kai blinked. "How's that again?"

His big hands shook her gently. "Don't you understand? We go great together! You like to fish, you even play chess! You're just like Ken. It's as if he were here with me."

She wasn't sure whether that was a compliment. After all, she was a female! Her chin tilted. "I'm not Ken," she snapped.

"You're prettier. You're softer. You're—well, you're something I've never had much to do with."

His eyes were locked with hers, and she could not turn away.

Her heart was hammering. Why did he have this effect on her? She ought to twist away, keep her distance. He could shift his hands to her throat, and then she would be a goner. Yet she could not move.

"I'm just a girl," she breathed.

"You're much more than just 'a girl'! You're something special, something I never believed could exist."

"Just because I like to fish?"

"Of course not. You're so beautiful. . . ."

His words trailed off. But his eyes were speaking to her, telling her that he thought she was the most exquisite thing God had ever made. Kai wished her heart would take it easier. It was slamming and bumping away between her ribs as though it sought to wrench itself free.

Her tongue seemed glued to the roof of her mouth. She could not free it to talk. All she could do was stand here and—well, she was not exactly standing, she was inching forward toward him, as if her muscles were obeying something in her that had taken over her body.

Now she was practically leaning against him. Her arms were up, her hands spread on his shoulders. And his arms were about her middle.

In another moment. . . .

"Lunch," she breathed.

"What? Oh! Oh, yes. Lunch."

He freed her so swiftly that she almost fell forward. Drat! Why had she mentioned lunch? She wasn't at all hungry. Is that all that was needed to scare him off? A mere word? Her lips curled. He would certainly make a lousy lover!

What am I thinking of? A lover! Fate forfend!

Yet she felt angry, as though he had pushed her aside. Ignored her. She went to the refrigerator, got out some luncheon meats, tossed them on the counter. When he started to take bread out of the breadbox, she elbowed him aside.

"I'll make the sandwiches," she muttered.

"Have I said something I shouldn't?" he asked.

Kai eyed him sideways. She wanted to yell at him, to tell him that when he took a girl in his arms, he ought to kiss her. Not abandon her because she told him it was time to eat!

She slammed sliced ham on bread, then reached for the mustard. Somebody ought to take him in hand, tell him that when he wanted to kiss a girl, he ought to. Not yank away as though she had the mumps. She slapped mustard on the ham, angrily.

"I have offended you. I can tell. I'm sorry."

Her shoulder lifted and fell. "Don't be an idiot!"

His hand caught her, turned her. "Come on. No secrets. Tell me."

She could not meet his eyes. "Oh, go take your sandwich and sit down."

His grip tightened. "Not until you tell me. If I did anything, if I said anything, I'm sorry."

"You didn't do anything," she muttered.

That was true enough.

"I did. I don't know what it was, but. . . ."

His hands tightened, holding her helpless. He breathed, "Is that it? Can that be it?" There was a note of intense gladness in his voice.

His hands pulled her forward.

"Let go of me!" she yelled.

"Oh, no. No, indeed, my darling."

"I'm not your——"

His kiss caught the words on her mouth, mashed her lips. His arms were all but breaking her back, he was holding her so close to him that he could surely feel every imprint of her flesh. Against her will, Kai felt her mouth loosen, open. The touch of his tongue against her own made her senses swim.

She clung to him. A tiny voice whispered caution to her. She ought not be doing this. Roderick Grant was nothing to her, she was nothing to him. Yet she paid that tiny voice no heed. It was almost as though she were starved to be held and kissed this way.

He let her go, after a long time, yet his hands still held her.

"Look at me," he whispered.

Kai opened her eyes, stared up at him. Her senses were swimming, she was so weak she would have fallen if he had not maintained his grip on her.

"I love you," he said in an astonished voice. "I really love you!"

"You're nuts!"

"No, I'm not. And you love me. Come on, admit it."

"I hate you. You—you—you tried to kill me."

He kissed the tip of her nose. His lips went from her nose to her cheeks, to her forehead, to her chin. Oh! Now he was kissing her throat and his lips were like a pleasant fire along her flesh.

She had to stop this. If she didn't, she would be urging

him into the nearest bed. But how could she stop it, if her body didn't obey the commands of her brain?

Then he kissed her forehead and pulled away, saying, "What kind of a heel am I, taking advantage of you like this? Here you are, alone with me, and I'm supposed to protect you."

Take advantage of me! Take advantage!

He guided her to a chair, eased her into it. "Don't let me do that again, Kai. I won't be responsible. I can't be. You can't understand how weak I can be where you're concerned."

She was still too shaken to do anything but nod her head. She whispered. "I'll try."

He put the sandwiches and the coffee on the table and sat down opposite her. "Eat. Then we'll play chess."

To her surprise, she began wolfing down the sandwich, looking anywhere but at Roderick Grant. She did not dare meet his eyes. Not yet. Maybe in a little while, but right now she had to have some time to think this thing out.

She could not have fallen in love with him. She denied that to herself, vehemently. It had just been a physical attraction, a thing of the moment. She would have acted that way with any man, being off with him alone like this. It wasn't Rod, at all. It was her fault, she would have to be more careful.

After a time, she came back to something like normality.

Playing chess would be a good thing. It would require her to devote all her attention to the game, she wouldn't be able to think about those kisses and what they did to her. She would show Roderick Grant that she would make a good opponent for him. Ha! Even better than that. She would beat him.

Yet they dawdled over second cups of coffee.

"If you don't know of anyone who wants you dead," Rod said suddenly, "then why were you attacked?" Not waiting for her to answer, he went on, as if to himself, "It may be something you saw, down there in the sea. Did you see anything, Kai?"

"Of course I did. Shells and mollusks, some coral, a lot of sand."

He gestured impatiently, and Kai smiled to herself. Good! I've annoyed him. And I intend to keep on annoying him, too. If only to keep him from making free with me!

Sure! Cut off your nose to spite your face.

"I'm serious, Kai! You had to have seen something, something that's dangerous for you. So dangerous, that man was ready to kill you to keep you silent."

"You're ridiculous."

He shook his head slowly. "No, I'm not. I saw that man. He had on diving gear. Good stuff, too. Now, no homicidal maniac is going to swim along the bottom of the ocean hoping to find a victim down there. It's against all reason. Even crazy people don't do things like that."

"But what reason would a man like that have to kill me?" she asked patiently. She may as well be patient with him. Humor him.

"That's what I'm trying to find out. You saw something. Or that man thinks you saw something. Something dangerous enough for you to make him want to get rid of you."

"But what could I have seen? It doesn't make sense."

"How about that treasure you're after?"

Kai scorched him with a look. "Do you think I'm a complete ninny? I was looking for treasure, for a sunken ship—or some part of it. If I'd have seen it, I would certainly know about it."

"That makes sense. Then it was something else. But what in the world could be down there on the ocean bottom that would be so deadly to anyone who might chance to come upon it?"

"There was nothing, I keep telling you."

"What you mean is, you didn't see anything. Nothing suspicious, that is." He brightened suddenly. "Say! Maybe that man who tried to kill you found the treasure you're looking for—and intended to kill you to make sure you didn't tell anyone."

Kai sighed. Really, this man was too much! Couldn't he understand plain English? She said slowly, "Listen to me. I've hunted other treasure ships. I know what they look like.

"Ever since I was a little girl, it seems, I've been skin-diving along the bottom of the ocean with my brother. If there were a sunken hull down there, I would have seen it." She raised her voice. "I would have seen it! Can't you get that through your head?"

Rod chuckled. "Okay, okay. I must be making a nuisance of myself. No more talk about diving or treasures or anything else. Agreed?"

When Kai nodded, he asked, "Then how about some chess? We have the whole afternoon, we ought to be able to get in several games."

While she washed and dried the dishes, Rod set up the chess board. It was a handsome board, it looked to be made of teakwood. As he opened the box that held the chessmen and lifted them out, one by one, Kai paused in the drying of a cup and stared. They were of ivory and ebony, and looked handcarved.

Would a man who played chess casually have such a set?

She regarded him thoughtfully. Maybe the guy was a chess wizard. If so, she wouldn't have much of a chance with him. Mentally, she gritted her teeth. Ha! She herself was no slouch. She had beaten her brother again and again. If Ken could give him a good battle, maybe she could beat him.

Kai sat down with confidence stirring in her. When Rod gestured for her to start, she moved her knight's pawn to the knight's fourth square. Rod reached out to slide his king's pawn to the king's four.

To counter this, Kai advanced her bishop's pawn one square.

Rod sat back in his chair and smiled at her. "You don't want to do that," he said softly.

"Of course I do."

He shook his head. "I'll let you take that move back."

Faintly troubled, Kai studied the board. Everything seemed serene; after all, it was only the start of the game. She snapped, "My move stays."

Rod sighed, then moved his queen to her king's bishop four.

"Checkmate," he said softly.

Kai stared at the board. There was open space between her king and Rod's queen. Two empty squares. And—there was nowhere to move her king.

Anger stirred in her. "You cheated!" she snapped.

His eyebrows rose. She decided she hated him when he did that, as though he were in the classroom and one of his students had said or done something especially stupid. Her hands clenched into fists.

"That wasn't fair," she muttered.

"All's fair in love and war, and chess is basically a war game."

Oooooh! He sounded so—so professorial! She hated him all the more. Now he would probably lecture her about chess, about its beginnings, about its history.

His eyes were twinkling, she noted. Oh, he was probably very amused at her—her stupidity. Well! She would show him. "Another game? If we can call that a game, that is."

"Of course. Your move."

Kai rearranged her pieces, then bent over the board, frowning. What attack ought she make? Obviously, Rod was no beginner. If she ever hoped to beat him, she had to think. And—think hard.

Her hand reached out.

An hour later, she was down to two pieces. Rod only had two pieces left, his king and a knight. She still had her queen—the most powerful piece on the board—and, of course, her king. She was going to win this one. There was nothing Rod could do to stop her. All she had to do was eliminate that knight, then her queen would pin his king and the game would be over.

Rod moved his knight. "Check," he said softly.

Kai lifted her hand to slide her king out of danger when she realized the trap Rod had set up. True, her king was in check, but if she moved her king, Rod would take her queen!

"It's what is known as a forking check," Rod smiled.

"You have to move your king. I take your queen. It's the beginning of the end."

She glared at him. Why must he be so superior? It wasn't fair! Her lower lip began to tremble. She had been so sure of herself! She had felt she had him on the ropes. In one move, he had shattered her.

"Phooey," she breathed.

Tears came into her eyes. Roderick Grant was a—a *bully!* He must have known how badly she wanted to beat him. He could have let her.

"I hate you," she told him. "Hate you, hate you!"

"Hey, it's only a game."

She was beyond words. Didn't the big oaf understand that this was more than just a game to her? It was a battle of wits, of brains. And he had clearly outclassed her.

"Come on. One more. I'll let you win."

That did it. Kai jumped to her feet, weeping openly now, hands clenched into fists. Tears ran down her cheeks, but she didn't care. Let him see her like this. What difference did it make?

"You're a big b-bully! That's what you are—a b-bully!"

He was out of his chair and standing before her almost before she was aware of it. His arms went around her and brought her in against him, holding her tightly.

"Don't cry. I can't stand it when you cry. It does things to me."

"Wha-what k-kind of things?" she blubbered.

"It tears me up inside. It hurts."

"G-good! I'll cry and cry and——"

He kissed her, then, lifting her face with a finger under her chin and applying his mouth to hers. Kai told herself to pull away, to yank herself free and lash out with her fists. Hit him and hurt him! Make him suffer! Yet all she could do, she found, was lean into him and let him feast on her lips.

"No," he was saying against her lips. "I don't want you to cry. I want you to laugh and sing and enjoy life. That's what someone like you was made for. To do anything else would make you a traitor to what you are."

If only his arms were not so strong! If only his kisses were not like sweet fire when they rained down on her mouth! If only she did not like being held and hugged this way! What in the world was the matter with her? She hated it when he held and kissed her. Why then, did she permit him to do it?

Now he was wiping away her tears, smiling down at her.

"I wish you wouldn't do that," she said as coldly as she could.

"Wipe away your tears, you mean? But I enjoy it. Though I don't like to see you cry."

"You're the one who makes me cry," she flared.

She was positive that look of horror and dismay on his face was pure theatrics. He was no more sorry for what he had done than was the chair he had been sitting on.

Kai stared up at him, suddenly aware that he really hadn't done anything, except beat her at chess. She had never carried on like this when Ken beat her. What was the matter with her, anyhow? She was like a weathervane, swinging this way and that before the slightest puff of Roderick Grant's actions.

"What must you think of me?" she gasped. "I'm acting like a spoiled child!"

His faint grin touched something inside her and she giggled. Next moment she was laughing hilariously, staggering about, then collapsing into a chair. Reaching for a handkerchief, she wiped her eyes.

"I haven't laughed like that in I don't know how long," she told him.

"It's good to hear you laugh."

Kai frowned. "I've never had too much to laugh about."

"Sure you have. You just haven't realized it."

"Oh? What makes you say that?"

"First of all, you're beautiful."

"I'm not!"

"But you are," he went on gently, smiling at her from where he sat on an ottoman almost at her feet. "Beautiful and smart and athletic. How much better can a girl be? You also play a very good game of chess."

"Now there you're wrong. You beat me twice."

"I've played a lot of chess. I've even won prizes at it. You gave me a fine game after that first one." His eyes were laughing, inviting her to laugh with him.

Kai grimaced ruefully. "I was stupid to fall into that trap. A fool's mate, I think you call it?"

"It's also known as the 'hara kiri' game. You just weren't paying attention."

That was true enough, she realized. She had thought to sweep Rod off the board with some brilliant stratagem, and had been caught up short. Oddly enough, she found that she did not mind it, now. Rod had warned her, hadn't he? He had offered to let her take her move back. If she hadn't been so pigheaded, she would have seen that trap.

"Next time I'm going to beat you," she warned.

"Good. We'll play again, right after dinner."

Kai relaxed, stretching out her legs, crossing them at the ankles. It was so pleasant here, she could not remember a time when she had enjoyed herself more, or had been more at ease.

Could this be because of Rod?

Kai wondered.

Five

THE DAYS SLID away, one after the other, each one more pleasant than the last. Kai became aware that she was happier than she had ever been. She had lost her suspicions of Rod—at least temporarily—and was flinging herself into this holiday with every atom of her being.

It was fun to fish with Rod, to sit there and watch him as he poled his pirogue along the waterways of the Everglades, past tropical hammocks with their stands of exotic shrubs and trees. Rod would call out their names to her at times, indicating strangler figs, pigeon plums, and paradise trees. She would always marvel at his knowledge, which he invariably shrugged off.

"I've lived here for years," he told her. "These lonely places are like my own backyard, so to speak. Even when I was a youngster, my father brought me here. I've made friends with some of the Seminoles whose reservation is close by."

Kai sighed. "It's like a world apart."

It was a world she would like to become a part of, she knew. Something inside her responded to the quiet, to the loneliness of these vast tracts of watery realms. If only she could stay here forever!

Of course she couldn't do that. She was only here because Rod and her brother had some crazy notion that her life was in danger. Still, she was grateful, no matter what the reason. She breathed deeply of the air, her eyes drank in the sights of torch wood and bustic trees, she watched as a flock of flamingos fed, their plumage pink in the brilliant sunlight.

There was the time—it was the third day she had been here—when Rod had slowed the pirogue and called her attention to a little hummock past which they were gliding. He did not speak, but pointed, and when Kai followed his finger, she saw tree snails clinging to or moving about three trees.

Their shells were exquisite, being a blend of riotous colors that almost took away her breath. There were bands of orange and brown and gold, of blue and black and gold, together with gold and white, with black and gold and white. Each shell was a tiny masterpiece, and Kai reveled in their sight.

"They're breathtaking," she enthused.

"Whenever I find an empty shell, which isn't often, I pick it up and carry it back to the cabin. I have a small collection. I'll show it to you tonight."

He dug in the pole and the pirogue glided on soundlessly through the water, but Kai turned and stared at the snails until they faded from view.

Then came the morning when she opened her eyes to the sound of a motorboat chugging along. Kai wriggled a little in bed, enjoying the warmth and the knowledge that she was going to have another day with Rod. Lazily she threw back the covers, slipped out of bed to stand a moment, staring out the window.

There was a motorboat, and it was being driven by a woman with pale blond hair. Kai froze, staring. The Chris Craft was turning toward the cabin!

She leaped for her clothes, snatching up a pair of shorts and a blouse. Who was the blonde? What was she doing here? Could she be someone who knew Rod well? In other words, that girl friend he had talked about some days ago? Her fingers became clumsy, she could scarcely zip up the shorts.

Then she was out of her room, eyes searching for Rod. Yes, he was still here, cracking eggs into a bowl for the scrambling. Her heart slowed its furious pace.

In a casual voice, she announced, "You have a visitor."

He looked up, smiling his morning greeting at her. Then he shook his head. "Nobody comes here. You must be mistaken."

"A blonde," she murmured coldly. "In a Chris Craft."

"Not—oh, Lord!"

He dropped the eggshells and ran. Kai ran after him, to the door of the cabin, where she slowed her headlong pace to lean a shoulder against the jamb and watch as Rod strode toward the water's edge where the Chris Craft was stopping. The blond girl waved both arms at Ron.

"Darling! Surprise! I've come to drag you out of your hermit's hut and back to life."

Rod said something—Kai didn't quite catch it—and the blonde replied, "Darling, be sensible. You can't hide yourself away forever."

Kai seethed, listening to that honeyed, sirupy voice. It was almost nauseating. Apparently Rod didn't think so, because he was extending a hand to the blonde, lifting her up and over the gunwale and putting her feet down on grass.

Her arms went around him. Around his neck as a matter of fact, and they were dragging his head down to her waiting lips. Rod put his arms about her and met her mouth with his own.

Kai saw red. She quivered, she felt an angry flush that seemed to rise up from her feet through her entire body, and shook to its progress. Who was this floosey? What gave her the right to treat Rod as a—a lover?

As the blonde broke away from Rod to lean back and smile up at him, Kai felt her heart drop. She was lovely! Breathtakingly beautiful! Her eyes wandered over a complexion that would have put the petals of a rose to shame, over moist red lips, over long blond hair that was so golden it was almost white. Slowly her gaze ran over full breasts, rounded hips, and sleekly plump thighs.

How can I compete with something like that? Beside her, I'm a frump!

Compete? Now why should she think that? Roderick Grant was nothing to her. He was her brother's friend, that was all. Just the same, it didn't help her ego to have a golden goddess come along and throw herself into Rod's arms.

Of course! This was Sandra Alberts. The *rich* Sandra Alberts, whose family owned half the state. It had to be.

Under scowling brows, she watched Sandra link her arm with Rod's and walk him toward the cabin. Her voice was melodious, too. She spoke in something like a song.

"I had Joe run the boat down here for me, angel. I've come to visit for a few days. Unless I can talk you into coming back with me. You see, I want——"

Her words broke off and Kai found herself being stared at in something like astonishment.

"Rod! You naughty boy! I never thought you had it in you!"

The naughty boy was squirming in something between embarrassment and agony, Kai was pleased to see. His face was red—even under his tan—and he did not look at her.

"Kai is here as—as protection," he managed to say. Then, apparently recollecting himself, he added, "Kai, this is Sandra Alberts. Sandra, Kai Pierce."

Kai nodded her head, muttering, "Hello. Glad to meet you."

Oh, what a liar I am!

Sandra exclaimed, "I must have a good look at you. Really, I must. I've never known Roddy to admit a female to his holy of holies. Even *I* was shaking when I pulled up. I didn't know whether he'd throw me in the water or not."

Her blue eyes were sparkling with laughter. And with something else, Kai realized. Anger? Subdued fury? Yes, that was it. Sandra Alberts was seething with rage. And jealousy. Oh, yes. Kai could recognize those emotions very clearly, because that was how she was feeling herself.

She was being scanned very thoroughly. Those eyes were raking her from head to toes, taking her all in. Apparently Sandra did not like what she was seeing, because there was a tiny frown on her formerly smooth brow. A frown which she was hiding from Rod because all he could see of her was her back.

Astonishment held Kai for a moment. Surely she was mistaken. This vision of delight—in shorts by Giorgio Armani (that revealed sleekly lovely legs) and an almost sheer blouse by Gianni Versace—could hardly be jealous of *her!* Especially in the rumpled things she had yanked on when hurrying out of bed.

Sandra put laughter on her full mouth as she swung back toward Rod. "What are you protecting her from, darling? Not yourself, or you wouldn't have her holed up with you like this!"

Kai heard the anger and the suspicion in her voice. Which Rod could not, of course, being a man. Suddenly the mischievous imp that lived deep inside her, and of whom she had been ignorant until very recently, sprang to life inside her.

"He's just testing his willpower, Sandra," she said sweetly. "He invited me here to test his inner strength. As a sort of bet, you might say. He isn't to grab me and kiss me."

Icicles dripped from her words as Sandra murmured, "Oh? Willpower?"

"He's pretty good, too," Kai answered as if grudgingly. "He's only kissed me half a dozen times in the last day or two. I think that means he's in control of himself, wouldn't you?"

Sandra glared at her. Kai glared back.

That was when Rod said, "We were just about to sit down for breakfast, Sandra. Now you can join us."

"I really don't think I should intrude on this little paradise for lovers!"

"Oh, Kai's only having fun. We're here because somebody tried to kill her. Nobody can find her away out here."

Sandra looked hard at Kai, who understood that if someone were to come along and murder her right at this moment, Sandra would probably lend a helping hand. There was a challenge in that look which told Kai very clearly that if she wanted Roderick Grant, she was going to have to steal him from Sandra Albert's clutches.

As if to prove this, Sandra caught Rod's arm in both of hers and began walking him toward the cabin. "Breakfast sounds divine, angel. I haven't tasted your cooking for too long a time."

Almost grudgingly, Kai stepped back from the doorway to let them enter. As Rod went by, she swung her foot, kicking him on the shin. When he turned a pained face toward her, Kai said sweetly, "I'm so sorry. I must have stumbled."

Sandra seated herself in Kai's chair. When Rod went to fetch another one for her, Kai gave him a black scowl and caught up a chair before he could put his hands on it.

In a voice that she pretended to be trying to keep low, but made certain that Sandra could hear, she said, "You know you promised to make love to me all day today. Get rid of her."

As Sandra's face flamed red, Kai smiled at her very sweetly, then murmured, "You'll have to forgive me, but I have to make the coffee. Rod adores the coffee I make. He calls it the nectar of the gods."

The look on Sandra's face was reward enough for everything that had happened this morning. Humming gently, Kai picked up the coffee can and the percolator, and set about brewing godlike nectar.

She had been so busy scoring on Sandra that she had not noticed Rod's reaction to her words. Now as she stood beside him, measuring out coffee while he scrambled eggs, she heard him say softly, "If I'd known I made that promise, I'd have chased her out of here."

Kai flushed to the roots of her thick brown hair. Drat! What had made her say such a thing? Now she supposed that as soon as Sandra left, he would try and hold her to it. Ha! Big fat chance! She was one woman who made love to no man.

And yet. . . .

She began to dream, standing there before the percolator. She had never been made love to in her entire life. What would it be like? Remembering the manner in which Rod had caught hold of her and kissed her, a tiny part of her was whispering that she would enjoy it very much. She certainly had loved those kisses! Even if she had fought against them.

Hmmm! Some fight she had put up, leaning into him and letting him hold her as though she were drowning and he were trying to rescue her. Letting him kiss her all he wanted was bad enough, but she had a vague memory of having put her arms about him and hugging him at the same time she was pretending not to want those kisses.

Oh, well. In another day or two she wouldn't be seeing Roderick Grant any more. She was safe enough now. If anybody had really wanted to kill her, as Rod had claimed, they had probably lost all interest in her by this time.

As the coffee began perking, Kai felt unease touch her. The realization came to her that she did not want to leave this Everglades cabin, that she had never been happier in her life than during these all-too-few days, alone here with Rod. What would it be like to go back to a life where there was no Rod to greet in the morning, to make coffee for, to fish with, and—yes, and to play chess with, too.

Of course, she had only won one of those chess games—and she had a sneaking suspicion that he had let her win—but it had been so much fun, sitting together over the chess board, staring down at the pieces, knowing that Rod was within touching distance all the time. Now why was that? She had played chess with her brother often enough, and with him there was no feeling of rapport, of togetherness, of something more than mere companionship.

Strange!

Then Rod was serving the scrambled eggs and ham slices, the toast, and she came to fill the coffee cups. Out of the corner of her eye, she noted that Sandra had almost casually slid her chair closer to Rod, that she was only toying with the food on her plate.

"Daddy wants to see you, Rod darling," Sandra was saying. "He wants to talk to you about a partnership in some venture or other." The blue eyes turned from Rod to Kai. "My father wants Rod in one of his many firms. He feels Rod is being wasted, teaching in the university.

"Rod has a brilliant mind. He could be making a fortune in industry. Instead, he only earns peanuts as a professor."

Kai nodded. "I'm sure of it. But then, he's happy doing what he is, and that's the most important thing there is. Being happy, I mean." She smiled sweetly. "Rod is very happy right now. Or was—until a little while ago."

She sighed dramatically. "I wonder if you can understand how lonely it is here in the Everglades, at this cabin. Oh! Not lonely for us! We have each other, Rod and I. When there's no one around to spoil our little paradise. Or—wasn't."

She could actually hear Sandra gritting her teeth.

Sandra said almost shrilly, "Rod could make a fortune in business with my father."

Kai shrugged. "Oh—money. Pooh! What's money beside exquisite happiness?"

The golden goddess glared at Rod, who devoted himself to his ham and eggs. Then, very slowly, her scowl disappeared and a faint smile touched the corners of her mouth.

In an overly sweet voice, Sandra murmured, "I had intended to bring Rod back with me—to our family mansion." She sighed. "I guess I won't be able to do that now, of course. So I'll have to sleep here." She reached out a hand toward Kai. "But I won't interrupt you two lovebirds. I'll sleep in the spare bedroom."

Kai gulped. She opened her mouth to protest that it would be her bedroom Sandra Alberts was taking, but snapped it shut. Where would that leave her? Certainly not with Rod! She wasn't going to go to bed with him! If he started kissing her. . . .

Rod said, "Relax, you two. There's no problem. You have your room, Kai. Sandra can sleep in my bed."

"Whaaat?"

Kai flushed. She hadn't meant to yell like that. It had just come out, spontaneously. Then she saw Rod's sly smile.

"I only meant that she could have my bed. I'll sleep in

the living room. The couch opens up into a bed. We can all get a good night's sleep."

How could she get across the fact that she didn't trust Sandra Alberts as far as she could throw her? She wouldn't put it past the golden goddess to come out of her room and slide into the Castro convertible with Rod. Hmmm. She would have to stop that, in some way.

Now why should she care what Rod and Sandra did together? It meant nothing to her. She certainly had no claim on Roderick Grant. Just the same, she wasn't about to let it happen. Ha! Lie alone in her bed while Sandra and Rod made love together in the living room? No way!

"I'll do the dishes," she stated, as she rose to gather up the plates and cups. She might as well let Rod see that Sandra Alberts was no homemaker, that she was lost when it came to caring for a man.

Sandra leaped up. "I'll wash. You can dry."

Kai gritted her teeth. "You aren't used to doing dishes. I'd better clean them."

"I'll have you know I'm no pampered pet, girl. I've washed a lot of dishes in my time. My father doesn't believe in spoiling his only child."

Rod chuckled. "We'll all do them. I'll wash. You girls can dry. And for Pete's sake, relax. While we're here, we might as well enjoy each other. Have a good time together."

Both girls swung about and glared at him.

They finished the dishes in a deep silence, broken only by the running water, the soft rubbing of towels over cups and dishes. Only when they were hanging up the towels did anyone speak.

"I didn't bring any pyjamas, Rod," Sandra said thoughtfully. "I'll have to sleep in my undies—such as they are."

"I can loan you some pyjamas."

"No. They'd swim on me. I'd be more comfortable in my underwear or perhaps in nothing at all."

A vision of Sandra in the buff swam into Kai's head. Ha! Suppose Rod needed something in his room? A sleeping pill or his shaving equipment? Kai wouldn't put it past the golden goddess to leap out of bed—stark naked, too!—and offer to help him find them. She would be at a distinct disadvantage, off there in her room all by herself.

She could leave her door open, to make sure she knew when Rod might decide to go looking for stuff. If he did, she would leap out of bed and offer to find them for him.

Rod asked brightly, "Well? What shall we do? Play some chess?"

Sandra scowled, which delighted Kai.

"I'd love to," Kai sang.

Rod got out the chess board and the pieces, set them up on a table. Kai pushed her chair forward, then saw that Sandra had ignored Rod's chair to push a bench forward to the other side of the table.

"I'll sit beside Rod and watch," she caroled.

She sat beside him, all right, glued up to him so that he must be able to feel just about every curve she had. And Sandra Alberts had plenty of curves. Kai had to give her that, no matter how grudgingly.

She could not concentrate on the game. She watched Sandra practically hanging onto Rod, putting her arm about him, resting her golden head on his shoulder, exclaiming in admiration every time he moved a piece. She made blunders in her play, she just could not bring her skill to bear.

It seemed to Kai that Rod was being affected too, by Sandra's closeness. He muffed several opportunities to score off her by removing her pieces when she had made stupid moves. So, then! He was not insensible to Sandra's charms. For some reason, Kai found that this annoyed her inordinately.

He was a man, wasn't he? And Sandra—no matter how she, Kai, felt about her—was a gorgeous hunk of female. There was no reason to hate Rod because Sandra's soft body was distracting him. Yet she did hate him. She did! She did! He ought to push her away, tell her go sit in a chair at the other end of the room.

The game dragged on. It seemed to Kai that Rod did not want to win, that he wanted her to beat him. But she could not bring her mind to focus on the game, she was too busy watching Sandra when she hugged Rod or gave him a little kiss when he had practically been forced to capture her knight or bishop.

Once she was aware that Rod knew what was going on. She caught him looking at her with that tiny twinkle in his eyes. Oh, he was no dope. He knew that she and Sandra were being bitchy toward each other because of him. And he was lapping it up as a cat lapped up cream.

Kai set her jaw. She was going to beat him. She was! She must put Sandra out of her mind, she must concentrate on her pieces. She leaned forward, studying the board.

That was when Sandra began undoing her sheer blouse, holding it open to fan herself. "It's really hot in here, isn't it?" she asked brightly.

She was wearing a black brassiere, if one could call that sheer, almost transparent piece of gauze a bra. It certainly showed an awful lot of her, and Kai had to admit there was a good deal to show.

There went her game. She was so furious, she could not concentrate, not at all. She did note that Rod kept his eyes on the board—after one quick look, that is—and that he seemed suddenly determined to put an end to the game.

Two moves later, he said, "Checkmate."

"You won, darling," Sandra gloated, smiling. "It was wonderful."

"No, it wasn't. I played horribly." His eyes accused Kai, as much as told her that she should have won that game in record time and that he was disappointed in her for not doing it.

That was when Sandra murmured, "My, it's actually stuffy in here. I could do with a nice swim."

Rod looked at her. "Did you bring a bathing suit with you?"

"Darling, of course. I bought one especially for this little trip."

I can imagine what it looks like! Two skimpy pieces of material! Just enough to cover her in the most important places.

Kai bit her lip, frowning. Sandra wanted to compare their bodies, of course. Well, she had nothing to be ashamed of. But where was there to swim, in these Everglades?

When she asked this of Rod, he chuckled. "I've put down wire fencing just off one side of the island. There's room enough to get wet, to cool off, anyhow. Shall we?"

Sandra squealed and ran from the cabin to get her suit.

Kai turned and looked at Rod, who shrugged, spreading his hands. "I certainly never figured on her showing up," he said.

"I'll bet you didn't," she snapped, and walked into her bedroom.

Fury made her tremble as she closed the door. So! He was actually flaunting his girl friend in front of her. Letting her see how gorgeous she was, how breathtakingly beautiful! Rich, also. Tears came into her eyes. Why couldn't she have been born rich, with the proverbial silver spoon in her mouth? Then she would be able to compete with Sandra Alberts!

She sat on the edge of the bed, glowering. It wasn't as if she loved Rod. He didn't owe her anything. He was merely a friend of her brother, someone who had come into her life out of nowhere. Actually, she hated him. Yes, that was it. She hated him.

Kai frowned. Well, that wasn't strictly true. She didn't hate him. Not really. She was indifferent to him, perhaps. Hmmmm. That wasn't quite right, either. But she was not going to compete with Sandra Alberts for him. Let the golden goddess have him, for all she cared.

Sandra was back in the other room, laughing and babbling. Kai seethed. She was playing up to Rod, flirting with him, probably flattering him. In a few minutes she would be going out to swim in something that a faint breeze would blow off her, showing her body to Rod, letting him know how gorgeous she was.

So let her. What did she, Kai, care?

There was silence outside. Sandra was most likely changing into her swimming things. Rod was in the living room. Or—was he?

Kai jumped up, ran to the door, and slowly opened it, peeking out. Yes, he was seated there, idly riffling through a magazine. Sandra was in his bedroom, about to don her swimsuit. His bedroom door opened suddenly and the golden goddess came out.

Kai caught her breath and her eyes went wide. The girl was positively stunning! Tanned all over, with a body that would have put Venus de Milo to shame, clad only in a couple of tiny things that didn't hide much of anything.

She closed the door and leaned against it, scowling. Was she going to let Sandra have Rod all to himself? Let her make up to him, hug him and kiss him, perhaps, or cling to him with that all but naked body in the water?

Rod was a man, and men were notoriously weak when it came to pretty girls who were all but nude. He needed some protection. He really did.

Kai reached for the swimsuit Rod had bought for her. It was a Roxanne, and fashionably brief. As she wriggled into it and adjusted the straps, she told herself it would show entirely too much of her. The mirror confirmed her opinion.

And yet....

She did look wonderful. She had great legs, too, and a slim middle, and her breasts bulged out the cups of the suit bra. She would not have to take a back seat to such a beauty as Sandra Alberts. If Rod wanted to look at female bodies, he could stare all he wanted at hers.

She stepped out into the living room. Sandra turned and eyed her up and down, and something in her eyes made Kai grateful that she had decided to go for a dip, after all.

"Have you known Rod long?" Sandra asked.

"Not even a week," Kai replied sweetly. "Of course, he's known my brother for ages."

"A week," the other girl murmured. "Not a very long time, is it?"

"How much is long—when two people attract one another?"

What else might have been said stopped as Rod came out of his bedroom, looking very big and brawny, tanned all over. His shock of pale blond hair was rumpled as though he had been running his fingers through it.

"Everybody ready?" he asked.

Sandra ran to him, put an arm about him possessively.

Staring up into his eyes, she whispered, "I've never been readier, darling."

Kai seethed, eyeing the closeness of their bodies. Sandra was certainly letting him know the shape of her body, the way she was pressing herself into him. He had put his arm about her middle, too, though Kai also noted that he did not hug Sandra as tightly as he did her.

Trying to pretend indifference, she walked past them toward the front door. The way she felt right now, she needed that swim, if only to cool the fever of her angry flesh. Rod brought Sandra after her, out into the hot sunlight.

Rod walked behind the cabin toward a sloping stretch of grass that ran down into the water. As she followed, Kai saw wire fencing running out into the water, forming a large rectangle that seemed clear of weeds, of fish.

"You're perfectly safe, swimming about in there," Rod was saying. "That fence is strong. Nothing can get in at you."

"What about alligators?" Sandra asked.

Rod grinned. "They never have yet."

The water shelved deeply, Kai saw. She poised a moment, then dove in. Cooling water embraced her, refreshed her as she clove through it to the surface and began swimming. Ah, this was delightful. Why hadn't Rod suggested that she and he swim here?

She turned, treading water, looking to see where Rod and Sandra might be. The golden goddess was clinging to Rod, actually rubbing her body against his, protesting at the coldness of the water, just getting her legs wet.

Kai sneered. Then she asked herself: What am I sneering at? Here I am all by myself, and Sandra has Rod in her arms and is playing up to him!

"Oh, don't. Don't," Sandra was pleading as Rod lifted her in his arms, preparatory to dropping her in the water. Ha! Now she was winding her arms about his neck, hanging onto him. At the same time, of course, she was practically caressing him with her body.

Rod lost his balance on the muddy bottom and tumbled forward, even as Sandra shrieked. Next moment they were in the water, and Sandra was laughing, hugging Rod, shouting that her suit was coming off.

Kai saw red. Hurriedly, she swam toward the others, coming up to them just as Rod regained his balance, standing and lifting Sandra onto her feet. A quick look reassured Kai. The golden goddess had not lost her suit, though the bra top was scarcely covering her.

"I'll hold Sandra up, Rod," she offered. "You go cool off with a nice swim."

Sandra glared at her. "I am perfectly capable of standing by myself, thank you."

Kai smiled. "Then why don't you?"

Rod cut in. "Hey, let's all swim, shall we?"

Without waiting for an answer, he whirled and dove. Sandra watched him go, then shrugged and dove herself. Kai watched her, telling herself that Sandra Alberts was like a fish in the water, as good a swimmer as herself. All that hanging on to Rod had been a great act.

Hmmmm! Two could play at that game.

Kai swam toward Rod. As she neared him, she cried out and doubled up. Instantly, his hands were catching hold of her, lifting her up and against him.

"What is it? What's wrong?" he asked.

His face was a study in anxiety, in worry. Kai clung to him—wriggling herself against him—and sobbed, "I think something bit me."

"Here, let's have a look."

He lifted her, carried her in his arms to the grassy bank, where he stretched her out and bent over her. Kai murmured, "My leg, Rod. Look at it. See if there's any blood."

While Rod examined her leg, Kai looked at Sandra, off by herself in the pool and looking mad enough to bite nails. Kai gave her a big smile. Then she turned back to Rod, who was taking his time with her leg, almost caressing it as he examined it closely, running his hands up and down its smooth length.

"I can't find a thing," he told her, after a time.

"I thought something bit me," she whispered. "Are you sure?"

"I'll check it some more."

Kai lay back and let him fondle her leg, reveling in the attention and in the knowledge that Sandra was beside herself with rage. If Sandra had not been here, she realized, she would no more have let him do what he was doing than——than she would jump into a pool filled with hungry alligators.

Rod looked at her, his blue eyes filled with laughter. "I think you're going to live. There isn't a thing wrong with your leg. As a matter of fact, it's a beautiful leg."

"It's just a leg," she whispered.

"Oh, no. It's a work of art. Just like all the rest of you."

They stared into each other's eyes, and Kai knew very well that if Sandra had not come wading out of the water right then, he would have taken her in his arms. What might have happened after that, she could only guess.

Sandra was scowling. "Let's sunbathe," she muttered, and lay down on Rod's other side.

The rest of the afternoon was spent beside the water, with the two girls glaring at each other, with Rod trying to make conversation. Even afterward, all through a steak dinner which Rod cooked, there was little talk. It was as if they were waiting for night to come.

They talked in monosyllables after dinner. Even Sandra Alberts seemed to have lost some of her spark. The evening dragged on.

At last, Rod stood up. "Time for bed, girls. I'll go get my things."

Kai made her move then. "No, no, Rod dear. I'll get your things. I know just where you keep them." She added as she went toward his bedroom door, "I certainly ought to, oughtn't I?"

There was a deep silence behind her, and Kai grinned and hugged herself mentally. That was one in the eye for Sandra Alberts!

She did not feel so triumphant when she went into her own room and closed the door. Just as she had put Rod's pyjamas and robe and slippers beside the Castro, Sandra had tugged at her blouse, then lifted it off completely. Then she had stretched, arms up and breasts out.

Rod, being a man, had stared. At least, for a moment.

Then he had averted his eyes and mumbled, "Guess we're all tired. A good night's sleep will do us all good."

Sandra, with her blouse over an arm, had leaned toward him, kissing him. She had whispered—just loud enough so Kai could hear—"If you get cold, darling, come in and snuggle up."

Then she had marched off triumphantly into Rod's room.

Kai had stormed into her room, so angry she was quivering. The nerve of that woman, undressing herself like that in front of Rod! And he had looked! That was what had so infuriated her. Couldn't he have closed his eyes when he saw what Sandra was doing? Or turned his back?

She ripped off her sweatshirt and threw it. She yanked herself free of her slacks and heaved them. Her bra and panties went next, sailing through the air. Then she was reaching for her pyjamas, the ones Rod had bought for her.

"The hell with them," she growled and leaped naked into bed. If Sandra were sleeping naked, she would, too.

And if the golden goddess came out naked to sleep with Rod—by golly! she was going to do the same thing!

Kai tried to stay awake, to listen to any sounds which might indicate that Sandra Alberts was sneaking out of her bed and into Rod's. She fought sleep as long as she could. Her eyes closed. She would just relax a little. . . .

She woke to the touch of lips on her cheek. Her eyes snapped open and she found herself staring up into Rod's blue eyes. She was opening her mouth to yell when he put his hand over her mouth.

"Ssssh! Talk in whispers, as I am."

"What are you doing in here!!!" she breathed furiously.

"Sandra's still asleep, so I grabbed this chance to tell you I've decided to take you back with me to see the police."

The police? What was he talking about? She grabbed the covers and pulled them up higher. Of course, he could see her bare shoulders—and the pyjamas lying unused on top of the bed—so he must be able to guess she didn't have anything on.

"What are you talking about?"

"I just wanted to warn you. Agree with everything I say."

He leaned down and kissed her mouth. Very softly, very gently, but—she could tell—with a lot of hunger. Then he was tip-toeing out of her room, closing the door behind him so carefully it made no noise.

Kai relaxed, the better to let her heart stop its mad banging, to ease the pounding blood racketing through her veins. Damn the man! How come he had this ability to all but knock her senseless when he kissed her or grabbed hold of her? She must watch that!

She slid from the covers and scowled at her dirty shorts and shirt. She was not going to appear in them again. Not with Sandra in her Versace blouse and Giorgio Armani shorts. Hey, wait a minute. Didn't she have a pair of Sasson short shorts that Rod had bought for her and she hadn't dared to wear?

Sure! Here they were, with this Geoffrey Beene blouse that was just as transparent as was Sandra's. Kai grinned. She would wear these things, if only to show Sandra Alberts that she wasn't the only girl around who had a good body.

Yet when she was clothed and staring into the mirror at her reflected image, she began to have doubts. She showed entirely too much of her legs. *Entirely* too much! And yet—hmmm. She did have great legs, and the shorts hugged her hips as a lover might. The blouse certainly was sheer enough, too.

Why not? Let Sandra see that she was not the frump she must have thought her yesterday. Show her that she was just as attractive as the golden goddess. Kai reached up to gather her long brown hair in an upsweep. A couple of tendrils hung down past her cheeks, but she liked the almost wanton look they gave her. She smiled and touched her lips with Norell bright-scarlet lipstick.

She walked out to join Rod in the kitchen. He turned at the sound of her footsteps and stared. His eyes took her in, from her shoes to her upswept hairdo, and they glowed.

"You're more beautiful than I had imagined," he breathed.

Her shoulder shrugged, but she had no control over the sudden surge of delight that ran through her. Maybe she could hold her own with Sandra Alberts, after all. Her mirror had not lied.

"I'll do the cooking," she announced.

"Nothing of the kind. You're a goddess, and a goddess must be served and waited on. You sit down and have some coffee."

She was turning toward the table when Sandra came out of Rod's bedroom. Her eyes went instantly to Kai, and she halted. For several seconds she stared, and Kai felt ecstacy erupt in her at what she could read in those eyes. She was not looking at the girl she had seen yesterday. This was an entirely different woman.

Self-doubt touched Sandra Alberts. But this she pushed aside as she came forward, saying, "So. We have a new day before us. What shall we do with it? Go fishing?" And to Kai, "I suppose he's taken you fishing with him?"

When Kai nodded, the other girl said, "I envy you. He's never taken me."

"Sit down and eat your breakfast," Rod ordered. "We're going back to town as soon as we've finished."

Sandra eyed him closely. "What's in town that's so important?"

"The police."

Sandra sat down at the table across from Kai, but she held her eyes on Rod. "Now what will you want the police for?"

Rod served scrambled eggs, toast, and strips of bacon. "I told you yesterday that Kai was here for protection. We even discussed why she needed that protection, remember? I told you, someone wants to kill her."

Sandra's eyes grew big.

She turned and stared at Kai, and to Kai's amazement, she could detect pity in those golden eyes that regarded her. "Now why should anyone want to kill you?" She smiled suddenly. "I would have wanted you dead yesterday, maybe—I was so jealous. But not really. At least, I don't truly think so."

Rod explained as they ate.

"None of us know why she was attacked, we can't think of any reason. But she was attacked, and we can't take the chance that she may be attacked again. Next time, they might succeed."

Sandra took a sip of coffee, then asked of Kai, "Don't you know any reason why you were attacked?"

"No. Absolutely none."

Sandra announced. "I'm coming with you, of course. Daddy has friends in high places. He'll help you."

Rod murmured, "Thanks, Sandra, but we don't want to broadcast our troubles to the world."

The golden girl pouted. "I can keep a still tongue in my head, Roderick. I may be rich and want my own way sometimes, but I'm not stupid. Besides—" and here she winked at Kai— "I want Kai to stay alive so I can steal you away from her. It's no fun to steal a man from a dead girl. So I want to keep her alive as well."

Rod looked at her, a little dazed. Kai smothered a smile. She knew what Rod was thinking. Women! he was saying to himself.

It was only much later that Kai remembered she had not denied the fact that Rod was her man. Sandra had thought so, obviously. Kai wondered why she had not denied it.

Six

THEY WENT THROUGH the Everglades in Sandra's Chris Craft, towing the pirogue. Kai had packed the suitcase Rod had given her, bringing along all the clothes he had bought, including the pyjamas. For some reason, those clothes had come to mean something to her; just what, she could not figure out, but she had no intention of leaving them.

Sandra drove the motorboat very competently. Eyeing her, Kai realized that she showed the result of having scads of money, quite obviously. Grudgingly, she had to admire her. A girl like that would make a marvelous wife for a man such as Roderick Grant. With her millions, he would never have to work again, he could spend all his time hunting for Atlantis.

Her lip curled. Imagine a grown man wasting his time doing a stupid thing like that! However, if he married into the Alberts millions, he would have to do something to occupy his time. Aside from making love to Sandra, that is.

Kai scowled. For some reason she could not understand, it annoyed her very much to picture Rod making love to Sandra. Ha! It more than annoyed her. It shook her up. But why? Rod meant nothing at all to her. If he wanted to bed down Sandra Alberts, let him. Yet she had to admit the thought of it actually hurt her.

Sandra was so beautiful. So competent! So sure of herself. By comparison, she herself was like the ugly duckling. Oh, she was good-looking enough, she supposed, though she had never thought of herself in that way. But she could never match Sandra when it came to money or clothes or sophistication. If Rod weren't the absent-minded professor type of person he was, he would have snatched Sandra Alberts into a marriage bed long ago.

Tears came into her eyes. Furtively, Kai brushed them away, dreading lest Sandra should see them. Or Rod either, for that matter. Woman-like, Sandra might well guess their cause. Rod, of course—being a man—would merely think she was frightened by thinking of someone who wanted to kill her.

As if there were anyone like that! It had all been a figment of Rod's imagination. She was not so positive now that Rod himself had tried to kill her. If he had wanted her dead, he'd had plenty of chances during those days when they had been alone at that cabin.

She glanced at him, saw him sitting there beside Sandra, enjoying this ride through the Everglades with the wind blowing his sun-bleached blond hair, his bronzed cheeks glowing with health, the muscles rippling all over his body when he moved.

She had to admit he was rather good looking. Strong, too, as well as being very well educated. In short, a perfect husband for some lucky girl like Sandra. Why hadn't he asked her to marry him? It didn't make sense. Yet the fact that he was still single pleased her in a way she did not understand.

He turned suddenly as though some instinct had told him she was staring at him. He smiled, saying, "This is the way to travel, isn't it?"

Kai nodded dumbly.

He would always be able to travel first class with Sandra, if he should marry her. Didn't the big dolt realize this? Why didn't he, then? Put a wedding band on her finger, and he had it made. Kai felt miserable.

In time, they came in sight of the landing where Rod had left his car. Of course, the car that had brought Sandra here was long gone, which meant that Sandra would have to ride with them. She would have to share Rod with the golden goddess. For some unknown reason, that fact irritated her.

Rod leaped from the boat, tying it to the little wharf that jutted out into the water, then he was turning to help Sandra out onto the wharf, then reaching out a hand to her, gripping her hand firmly, lifting her up to stand beside him. As though to help her maintain her balance, he slid an arm about her middle, giving her a little squeeze.

Kai melted into him, smiling up at him, whispering, "Thank you."

The fact that Sandra was watching them—and scowling, too—added to her appreciation of his little hug. But Sandra turned and moved toward the car, opening its door and sliding in onto the front seat. She turned and smiled at Kai, gloatingly.

Kai slid in behind her, onto a rear seat, gritting her teeth.

She was quiet as Rod got in and started the car, then eased it out onto the roadway. Sandra moved closer to Rod, snuggling up to him, saying, "This is like old times, Rod—you and I driving off somewhere to have fun."

"Except that it isn't a fun trip, Sandra."

Kai could have kissed him.

Sandra would not be quelled, however. "Oh, pooh. We'll drop Kai off and make a day of it."

"You don't understand. We have to see the police."

"Today? Now? Can't it wait?"

Rod said slowly, "You don't want Kai killed, do you? She may be murdered if we can't stop it."

Sandra didn't say a word, but her silence was eloquent.

No one spoke again, for the rest of the trip. Kai was smiling faintly, relishing Sandra's annoyed silence. Rod was concentrating on his driving, especially when they turned onto Route 1. He was maneuvering the car carefully, speeding up when he could or slowing as traffic stopped him. Then he was swinging to one side, and a few minutes later was stopping the car before Police Headquarters.

Inside the building, Rod inquired for Lieutenant Trent, and was advised that the officer was busy. "Just give him my name," Rod said. "And tell him I'm here to prevent a murder."

The officer at the desk looked surprised, but nodded. "Right away, professor. I know you're a good friend of his. But what's this about a murder?"

Rod gestured at Kai. "Somebody tried to kill her."

"He must be crazy," the man muttered, and reached for a phone.

Moments later, Kai was being ushered into an office where a desk was heaped high with papers and behind which sat a big man with wide shoulders, a thatch of red hair, and a harried expression on his face. At sight of Rod he got up and held out his hand.

"Sorry, Rod. I'm up to my throat in work. Somebody's been killing gangsters and we haven't been able to do a damn thing about it." He looked at Kai and Sandra, his worry and concern clear to see in his eyes.

Rod nodded. "Won't keep you then. But the other day, a man tried to kill Kai Pierce here. I was swimming along when I saw the attack and drove off her assailant."

Bill Trent sat down, after one quick glance at Kai, and murmured, "Tell me about it."

It was on the tip of her tongue to tell the policeman that it was Rod who had attacked her—or, at least, that she thought it was he. Instead, she listened as Rod described what had happened. When he was done, Trent eyed her.

"You got any enemies?"

"Of course not!"

"You're Ken's sister, aren't you? Thought so. Seems to me I've seen you here and there." He paused, then asked, "Anybody hate you?"

It was on the tip of her tongue to mention Sandra Alberts, but she decided against it. "No one. And I must say, I didn't see this attacker Rod mentioned."

Rod chuckled. "She thought I was trying to kill her. Probably still does, deep down."

A startled Sandra turned and stared at Kai. "Rod? Kill *you?* Why in the world should he?" She did not add that she wished he had killed her, but Kai could read it in her voice.

Lieutenant Trent smiled wryly. "One thing I can vouch for: It was not Rod Grant who sought to knife you down there. If he'd been trying, he would have succeeded."

Kai flared, "I outswam him to the surface."

The police lieutenant looked surprised. "Outswam Rod? I don't think so."

Sandra Alberts laughed out loud. "Darling, *nobody* outswims Rod."

Kai jutted her jaw forward. "If Rod is such a wonderful swimmer, why didn't he swim after this phantom attacker and stick his knife into him?"

"The only thing I was trying to do was save your life."

"Besides," Trent cut in, "it would have been murder for him to do that."

Kai felt properly squelched. She sat back in her chair, lifting a shoulder as if to shrug off this whole business.

Rod was saying, "Bill, I think we ought to go out to that same spot where Kai was diving. It just might be that the same man will be down there again."

"Don't be asinine! What would a killer be doing swimming around on the bottom of the ocean?"

Rod said quietly, "That's the very question I've been asking myself, off and on, ever since it happened. He was down there. I saw him. But *why* was he down there?"

Bill Trent looked hard at Rod for a long moment. "You have a point there. It doesn't seem at all logical, does it? He couldn't have known he'd find someone there unless he saw her dive over the side of her boat."

Rod shook his head. "No other boats anywhere around except my *Atlantis* and Ken's boat. That I saw, anyhow."

"Strange. Strange enough for me to look into it." He asked, "I suppose you want me to go out there with you, have a look around?"

"This afternoon. In my boat. I have enough gear for you. Kai will come, too."

83

It was on the tip of her tongue to tell Rod that she would not come. She was not yet over the fear that had been so strong in her that day. What did Rod want her to do, act as some sort of bait to get the killer to strike again?

That was when Sandra cried, "I'll come! I could do with a nice swim."

Kai scowled. She wasn't going to let Sandra go off with Rod and the lieutenant without her. No way. She gritted her teeth. She would go along on the boat, but she wasn't going in the water. Oh, no.

Rod stood up. "Let's get a move on, then."

"You go ahead. I'll catch up with you in a couple of minutes. Just want to let the boys know where I'll be."

Kai got to her feet. This time, Sandra was not going to have that front seat all to herself, with Rod. She began walking toward the door. Sandra came after her, but Kai lengthened her stride and made it to the car, sliding in on the front seat and giving Sandra a big smile.

"Looks like you'll have to take the back seat," she commented.

Sandra glared, then snapped, "Oh, shove over. The seat's big enough for the three of us."

Kai sighed. She couldn't refuse, not without making a scene. She slid over and Sandra got in beside her, scowling. Rod was already behind the wheel and Kai found herself pressed up against him.

She had to admit, if only to herself, that it felt good to be snuggled into Rod this way. It was a form of intimacy—she knew he could feel her hip, her shoulder—that she might have shied away from if Sandra had not been here. Oh, the golden goddess was aware of her and her nearness to Rod, she was making little petulant gestures, sniffing occasionally as though to tell Kai she realized that she had lost this opportunity, but that there would be others.

In a sweet voice, Sandra was saying, "I don't suppose you have one of my swimsuits on the *Atlantis,* Rod? No, I didn't think so. Oh, well—I can make do with a pair of panties and a bra, I suppose."

Kai could imagine Sandra Alberts in sea-wet bra and

panties. Ha! They would be like her skin, and utterly transparent. She herself had no second swimsuit to loan Sandra. Her own suit was on the *Dolphin;* it would take her only a minute or two to fetch it.

Then Rod said, "Sandra, this isn't a picnic we're going to. There will be danger down there on the ocean floor. I don't suppose it will make any difference to this mad killer if he stabs Kai—or you."

"Oh!"

Kai was aware that Sandra was sliding her eyes sideways to regard her. "Are you going to go diving with a kook down there waiting to run a knife into you?" Sandra asked. "You seem too sensible for that."

Rod thrust words between them. "Just because she's sensible, she's going to dive. How can we catch that would-be killer if Kai isn't there to bait the trap?"

There was glee in Sandra's voice as she said, "I get the feeling that your girl friend isn't at all anxious to go swimming. I think she's scared." In a softer voice, she added, "I don't believe I blame her, either."

"She'll be perfectly safe with me beside her."

Ah, but would she?

Kai thought about that for the rest of the trip. Only when Rod turned the Continental in toward the dock's parking lot did she stir. She would have to go get her swimsuit. There was no escaping that. She was not going to give Sandra a chance to sneer at her and mock her for a coward, no matter what it cost. Something might happen, too, which would prevent her from having to dive.

She ran when Rod parked the car, calling back over her shoulder, "I'll just be a minute."

There was someone on the *Dolphin* as she neared it, she saw. Then Ken loomed up, gaping at her, a rag black with oil in his hands.

"Where did you come from? Has anything happened? Where's Rod?"

She told him as she hurried toward her cabin with her brother all but stepping on her heels. "Rod seems to think that man will show up again if we go diving where we did the other day. He's invited along some police lieutenant he knows."

"Bill Trent?"

"That's the one. Here, give me a hand."

She reached for a duffel bag, tossing her suit and goggles into it, along with her Swimaster two-stage regulator. When she was reaching for her buoyancy compensator, Ken grabbed her wrist.

"Rod will have all those things on the *Atlantis*."

She shook free. "I prefer to use my own."

He sighed. "Still mad at him, eh? I thought those few days would teach you what a swell guy he is."

"He's all right. Th-there's another girl with him, somebody named Sandra Alberts."

"Oh, yeah. The rich one."

Kai could not help it. She turned to her brother, asking, "Is she—is he going to marry her?"

"Lord, no. She keeps after him, though, I give her that. Rod has never given her any encouragement, he tries to fight shy of her."

Her heart leaped excitedly. "Oh? She seems quite—well, assured of herself."

Ken grinned. "It's just her way. The poor kid's so damned rich, she expects everybody to fall down in a dead faint when she so much as notices them. She's really not a bad sort."

"Isn't she? I hadn't noticed."

She did not see the glee leap into her brother's eyes as she turned back to the bag, running the zipper closed. He pursed his lips thoughtfully, then nodded to himself.

As she carried the bag from the little cabin, Ken said, "Hey! I'm coming with you. I wouldn't miss this for all the treasure under the sea."

He came on her heels as she half ran along the dock toward the *Atlantis*. Rod was on the deck, talking to Sandra. He looked up as Kai and her brother stepped from the dock.

"Ken, good to have you aboard. Sandra, this is Ken Pierce. Ken, Sandra Alberts." Rod smiled at Kai. "I see you've brought your gear along. Good girl. We'll make a little holiday out of this."

Out of the corner of her eye, Kai noted that Ken was smiling at Sandra, and that the golden goddess was smiling back at him. Ha! Maybe Ken could keep the poor little rich girl busy, and out of her hair.

Rod was catching her by the arm, leading her along the companionway toward the cabins. There were three cabins, she noted, together with a spick-and-span galley. The *Atlantis* was spotless, she had to admit. It was a big cruiser, it looked large enough to cross the Atlantic if it had to.

Rod opened a cabin door. "You can change your suit in here. From now on, this is your cabin. Right next to mine." He paused, then added, "I hope this will be like a second home to you, Kai."

She saw a bunk, a dresser, a tiny chair. There were chintz curtains on the porthole, and the entire room, though small, was very attractive. There was a chintz bedspread on the bunk that matched the curtains.

Mentally, she compared it to her quarters on the *Dolphin*, deciding that this cabin was far lovelier. As she tossed her carryall onto the chair, she wondered how many other girls had ever used this cabin. Most especially, how often Sandra had slept in here.

"It's beautiful," she murmured.

"Now it is, now that you're here."

She wondered how a professor could afford to own a boat such as this. Then she recalled that Ken had told her about Roderick Grant and his dividends, his royalties, that he had money he didn't even know about.

"We'd better get up on deck," she said hastily.

"Not yet." His hands came to hers and gripped them. His eyes were kind, gentle, as he said softly, "I know we got off on the wrong foot, you and I. It's unfortunate that it happened the way it did. But now that we know each other, let's start over."

Uneasily, she muttered, "Sure, sure. Whatever you say."

His grip on her hands grew harder. "You're not listening. I love you, Kai. I love you so much that I watch you every chance I can get. And I know that you aren't any too anxious to dive down into the ocean with me."

"Oh, that's ridiculous," she breathed.

"Is it? Tell me the truth."

"We-ell, I *am* a bit nervous about it."

She looked up into his eyes, realizing that she knew, even before he acted, that he was going to put his arms around her. Oddly enough, she didn't pull away but let herself be drawn against him and held comfortingly, with both his powerful arms holding her closely.

"You brave darling," he whispered. "But don't worry. I wouldn't let anything bad happen to you. I'll be there with you, watching, guarding you."

"You're silly," she said against his chest, knowing her words were muffled. "Nobody wants to kill me."

"I surely hope not! But we'll see."

He turned her, bringing her out into the companionway with him, closing the door behind them. His arm was about her middle comfortingly, and Kai wondered at herself, asking herself why she did not pull free of him. It wasn't at all like her to let a man walk with her this way. The strange part of it all was, she enjoyed the sensation, very much.

As they came on deck, Kai saw that Sandra and Ken were sitting close together, talking away animatedly. It came to Kai then that her brother was rather handsome. He was tall and lean, heavily bronzed from sunlight, and appeared more animated than she had seen him in a long time. Her eyes slid sideways toward Sandra, and she would have sworn that the golden goddess had forgotten all about Rod and herself.

"Come on," Rod was saying. "You and I can run the boat. We'll start the engine, let her warm up until Bill arrives."

She climbed the ladder to the wheelhouse. Up this high, she could see out beyond the prow to the stretch of ocean straight ahead. The controls were highly polished, they glittered as if with newness. Apparently, Rod ran a tight ship.

Watching as Rod started the powerful diesel, she heard the throb and muted might of the big engine. She wondered if the engine were as clean and bright as the rest of the boat. Probably, she decided, eyeing Rod sideways. Rod was a man who liked to have everything as neat as possible.

When she heard voices, she turned and saw Bill Trent coming aboard, a small valise in his hand. He was shaking hands with Ken, now, smiling and nodding at Sandra, turning to wave up to them.

Rod said, "Okay, I'll take her out now. But you stay with me. I want you to get to know the feel of the *Atlantis*."

"Why should I do that?"

"I'm hoping that we'll be going out a lot in it, from now on."

Kai stood beside him for a time, during which he guided the cruiser out into the ocean, explaining that she was a seaworthy boat, that she liked to surge through the waves at top speed. She rode the waves easily, there was very little roll to her, and the engine had settled down to a muted thunder.

"You take the helm now," he smiled.

Kai had often steered the *Dolphin,* she didn't have to be told what to do. The *Atlantis* responded to her touch as easily as it had to Rod's. She realized that she was having a good time and that Rod standing beside her was a big part of her enjoyment.

"She's beautiful," she murmured.

She could feel the distant throb of the engine through the planking of the wheelhouse. The ocean was empty before her, and the prow was slicing easily through the waves. If only she did not have to dive down to the ocean bottom today, she would have been thoroughly happy.

Still! She would not be diving alone. Rod would be with her, and that police lieutenant and her brother would be on hand, ready to lend a hand if anything happened. She glanced sideways toward Rod, where he was studying a chart.

"We'll veer southward in a little while, about ten minutes. That should bring us close to where you were diving the other day. Keep navigating. I want a word with Ken."

Then she was alone on the bridge, with the wind blowing her hair, exulting in the delight of the moment. Everywhere she looked now, there was only sky and ocean. It was elemental out here, with the sea breeze gaining in intensity, gently balancing herself to the sway of the cruiser as it clove a path through the water.

She was happier than she had been for a long time, perhaps ever. Now why was that? Certainly not just because she was at the wheel of the *Atlantis!* It was a beautiful boat, yes; but she had steered other boats all over this section of the ocean.

Could it be because Rod was with her, telling her she was beautiful? No, certainly not. Then why? She tried to understand the reason behind her delight, and could not. Right now, even the idea of diving down along the bottom did not dismay her.

Rod came up the ladder, saying, "Not far now. Only about two or maybe three minutes more."

He held a pair of binoculars in his hand. He put the glasses to his eyes and studied the ocean ahead of them. "A couple of boats, here and there," he said. "They're probably fishermen. Nothing to worry about."

He waved to Ken then, who ran forward to release the anchor. Kai slowed the *Atlantis,* shut off the engine at his signal. The cruiser lifted and dropped to the surge of the waves as the anchor went overside.

"Into your swim things, Kai. I'll join you."

Sandra came forward as they stepped onto the lower deck. "Rod, let me come, too," she begged.

Her eyes locked with those of Kai, and Kai sensed the challenge in them.

"Sorry," Rod smiled. "This is serious business, Sandra. It isn't a fun thing. We want to see if Kai is attacked again, down there."

"Oh. Well then," she looked at Kai. "Good luck. Stay alive."

Kai trotted down the companionway, turning into the cabin Rod had assigned to her. Swiftly, she slid out of her clothes and into her two-piece swimsuit. Her heart was beginning to thump, she realized she was becoming very nervous.

If that man were down there, ready to stab her again! She swallowed as she lifted her mouthpiece and the

Swimaster regulator. She didn't know whether she would panic if she should see that killer. She realized that she was bait for the attack, but would she be able to go through with it?

Ken was watching for her as she came out into the open air. His eyes were concerned as he strode toward her. "You sure you're all right? You want to go through with it?"

Sandra was beside Kai, saying, "I'll go down in your place if you want me to."

Kai shook her head. "I have to do it."

But she was afraid. Oh, yes. She did not deny it, if only to herself. If there was a man down there with a knife in his hand, ready to run that knife into her. . . .

Kai shivered.

Then Rod was beside her, looking very powerful and sun-bronzed in his swimtrunks, with a diving knife strapped to his side, a buoyancy compensator strapped to his chest, his single cylinder backpack already in place. He was holding a back pack for her.

"Let's get going," he smiled.

They were all helping her with her gear, then. Even Sandra was kneeling, sliding the rubber fins on her feet over the neoprene boots as she lifted each foot. Rod was behind her, checking the straps to make certain they would not open on her once she got to the bottom.

His hand caught hers, drew her to the gunwale. They sat down side by side, and when Ken gestured, she flipped over backward, going down into the blue-green water, aware that Rod was beside her. The water closed over her head and she began to swim downward toward the bottom.

Down she went, ever downward, swimming steadily. She slid past a grouper and a bank of coral, into which a small school of grunts were darting. Her eyes took in the brightness of their silvery scales, the flirt and flap of their fins and tails. This was another world, down here, a world of eerie shadows, of brilliant colors.

Kai looked around her. Rod was nowhere in sight, though she turned completely around. Where was he? He could not have lost her! Panic surged up inside her. Blindly, she began to swim, as fast as she could move. If that killer was down here, he was going to have to catch her.

She swam on and on.

Seven

SLOWLY, HER FEAR fled away. As she swam, she kept turning and staring, seeing vast stretches of oceanwater, empty of all human life but for herself. There was no killer anywhere about, she seemed safe enough.

In the distance, she saw what appeared to be a stone wall, built of concrete. There were lengths of concrete—or what appeared to be concrete—piled here and there, one atop the other, though at crazy angles. Curious, she began to swim toward them. Veteran of undersea swimming, she had never seen anything quite like them.

A shadow touched her. Glancing upward she saw the lean whiteness of a blue shark gliding by, off to one side. Kai had learned that sharks are not the deadly attackers their reputations have made them out to be, but she was wary.

She swam on, though slowly, keeping her eyes on the shark which suddenly disappeared with a flip of its tail. Faintly relieved, Kai headed toward a stand of coral. A gorgeously colored butterfly fish swam into view, almost lazily. Where sea anemones swayed to the faint current, she could make out a couple of anemonefish, indifferent to the stinging tentacles of the sea anemones.

Somewhere around here she ought to find some indication of the wrecked *Santa Maria Gloriosa*. All she would need to be sure she was near the site of the sunken galleon was a bit of wood, barnacle-encrusted by this time, or perhaps a length of iron which would tell her where a cannon lay.

Kai went more slowly, exploring carefully.

It was then that she saw another swimmer moving toward her. She whirled, about to flee, when she recognized Rod. He was gesturing to her with a hand, pointing upward. Kai waved, swam toward him.

Her heart beat more strongly. Would Rod attack her here, unseen by any human eyes but her own? Was she over her fear of him? Yet he did not reach for his knife, instead he was merely treading water, waiting for her.

Then he was reaching out, catching her hand and squeezing it, pointing upward with his other. Side by side, they rose toward the surface.

As she popped into the air, she could not see the *Atlantis*. Instead, there was another boat not far off, with a black hull and a white superstructure, a cruiser as large as the *Atlantis*, with a number of men at the rail staring toward them. One of those men lifted something that caught the sunlight along it and pointed it at them.

The gunshot was loud over the ocean.

Rod yanked at her arm as he dove. Kai went down with him, swimming strongly. She had no idea of where they were in relation to the *Atlantis*—she must have swum quite a distance down there along the ocean floor!—but she realized that their lives were in danger.

Ah, but why? Why should anyone shoot at her? She had no knowledge that would threaten anyone! She was completely innocent of any wrongdoing that might prompt someone to shoot her for revenge. Who were these people who wanted her dead, anyhow?

Rod was swimming strongly alongside her. From moment to moment, he turned his head to look at her. With her inhalator in her mouth and with her goggles on, he could not read her expression, so she gave him a thumbs-up gesture to indicate that she was fine.

He tugged her upward and they surfaced once more. The black ship was quite a distance away now, and she could make out the *Atlantis* coming toward them at full speed.

Once more, Rod ducked under, bringing her with him. They swam toward the *Atlantis,* a few feet below the surface. The thought crossed Kai's mind that she was almost enjoying this experience with Rod. Oh, not the being shot at. No! But the camaraderie and the fellowship that was theirs as they fled from danger toward safety.

This time as they came up into the air, the *Atlantis* was nearby. They began their swim toward it. As Kai caught hold of the ladder, feeling Rod's hands on her thighs to boost her upward, he spat out his inhalator to ask, "You all right?"

She paused on the ladder to remove her own mouthpiece, to grin down at him and say, "I'm fine, Rod. Who were those men, anyhow?"

It was Bill Trent who answered her question as he aided her over the gunwale and onto the deck. "I'm not sure, but I'd be willing to bet they're Dolly Donati's boys."

Kai stared at him. "Who's Dolly Donati?"

"A Mafia man. You wouldn't know about him, because he keeps a low profile. Shuns publicity. But he has his fat thumb in a lot of the gambling and the prostitution rackets that flourish around here."

Rod was beside her now, water dripping from him onto the deck. He asked, "Now why should Dolly Donati want to kill Kai?"

Trent scratched his thick shock of red hair. "I haven't the faintest notion. It doesn't make sense. I'm going to have to have a little talk with Dolly." He paused, then looked hard at Kai. "You sure you're all right?" We heard a gunshot, and we headed this way."

Rod snapped, "She's not hit, but she can't be feeling any too happy. I'm not so happy myself." He caught her arm. "Come on, honey. Let's get down into the cabins and put some warm clothes on."

He helped her free herself from the oxygen tank, from the flippers. Then with an arm about her slender middle he guided her toward the companionway. Ken was up above, on the bridge, looking concerned.

Kai called to him, "Relax, I'm fine. Let's go home now, eh?"

Then Rod was moving beside her, squeezing her waist. He needn't squeeze her quite so hard, she told herself, but admitted at the same time that she did not mind being held so firmly. Of course, all she had on was the brief two-piece swimsuit and Rod was even more naked, with just his trunks.

As she was reaching for the knob of her cabin door, he swung her around to face him. Her eyes lifted to his face, seeing it grave, concerned.

"I'm proud of you," he whispered. "You're a brave girl. You didn't panic down there."

"You were with me," she smiled.

His arms were bringing her even closer against him, she noted. Pressing her body right into his, as a matter of fact. She should pull away, but she could not move. Those blue eyes of his were absolutely devouring her, hypnotizing her into immobility.

"I'm going to be with you all the time from now on," he said gently.

"Oh? What will Sandra say about that?"

His arms tightened even more. His lips came down on hers. Kai did not pull away. She joined her mouth with his in something like greedy hunger. She felt a vast surprise at that, before surprise was swept away by a wildfire that ran all over her flesh and pounded away fiercely in her veins. She trembled within his encircling arms. But not from terror. Oh my, no!

"I—I think you'd better let go of me," she breathed when he freed her lips. She was still nestled right up against him, encased by those strong arms, however.

"I don't want to let you go."

"Don't I have to get dressed?"

"Are you cold?"

Cold? Ha! If he knew how warm she was! If he knew that she wanted him to pull her into his cabin and lock the door and go on kissing her and never stop! Kai tried to tell herself that this would not do. Any more of this and Rod would begin to get the same idea.

Heaven help her then! Because she was not strong enough to push him away and deny her mouth—and other things—to him.

Rod kissed the tip of her nose, whispering. "Do you realize what an absolutely enchanting nose you possess? I could go on kissing it forever."

"Better than my lips?" she murmured, and could have kicked herself. What was happening to her? To the cool, calm Kai Pierce who looked down her nose at men?

He kissed those lips again, and after a few minutes he breathed. "Your lips are heaven on earth. Nothing less. They're like life itself to me. I could stay here forever with you."

"That's nice," she smiled, "but oughtn't we to put some clothes on?"

He grinned. "It's more fun this way."

"The others are expecting us," she pointed out in a small voice.

"I guess so," he sighed. "All right, then. I'll let you go put something on. But don't be long. I'll be waiting."

His arms eased their hold, freeing her. His hand went out to open her door. Kai found that she had to command her body to move, to take it away from his. It was a definite effort, she found.

Then she was alone in her cabin, turning to look at herself in the mirror fastened to the inner wall of the door. Her eyes opened wide as she eyed her reflection.

She looked like a hussy, with the bra part of her suit so loose her breasts were all but spilling out. No wonder Rod had been dazzled. Kai scowled, then laughed. So what if he did look? She wasn't at all bad-looking, this way, with her deep tan and her long legs, and her bellybutton showing above the lower part of her swimsuit.

Hmmmm. Never before had she posed before a mirror this way, never before now had she bothered about how she looked. She turned and walked, keeping her eyes on the glass. Yes, she had a fine figure, an excellent body.

Maybe a little large in the breastworks, but Rod seemed to like that. Her hips were plumply rounded, too.

She was just as enticing to men's eyes as was Sandra Alberts. She was positive of that. At least, Rod seemed to think so.

Rod was probably changing now. He would go up on deck without her and Sandra was up there. She would probably hurl herself at Rod, and. . . .

She had to hurry! Her bra top went one way, the pants another, and Kai dove for her clothes. She slid into the Sasson short shorts and the transparent Geoffrey Beene blouse. There! She was as clothed as she was ever going to be on this trip, especially with Sandra in her own shorts and blouse. Two could play at that game.

A brief study of herself in the mirror assured her that she had nothing for which to apologize. She looked absolutely eatable! Very tanned, very healthy, very beautiful. Let her thick brown hair hang down the way it was, sort of loose and wanton. It made her look extremely sexy.

Kai puzzled over that as she opened her cabin door. She had never cared to appear sexy. Just the opposite. She looked up to see Rod leaning against the bulkhead wall, clad in shorts and a T-shirt. His eyes glowed at sight of her.

"There ought to be a law against you," he smiled.

"A law? But why?"

"You're dangerous. You make a guy feel like falling down and worshipping you. You take away the breath, you're so lovely."

Kai flushed slightly at the adoration in his eyes. "I'm not so lovely," she murmured.

He caught hold of her—as she hoped he would—his eyes staring down into hers. "You're the loveliest thing God ever made. I never want to lose sight of you."

"Well, if you go on holding me like this, I guess you won't."

He was contrite, and his arms loosened. "Was I gripping you too hard? Did I hurt you?"

"Of course not. But we ought to go up on deck. Oughtn't we?"

"I suppose so," he answered somewhat glumly.

She went ahead of him along the companionway, knowing very well that his eyes were going all over her. As if in answer to that stare, she let her hips sway languorously. Though she had never done anything like that, she found it was very easy. Almost second nature.

They came up on deck to find Bill Trent and Ken sitting close together, talking quietly but earnestly. Sandra was above, on the bridge, steering the boat.

Ken looked up as they appeared, his face grave.

"Bill and I have agreed that you can't come home with me, Kai," he said. "We don't want to run the risk of your being shot down by one of those killers."

To her surprise, Rod chuckled. "Hey, that's no problem. Kai and I can stay together. I'll watch over her. I won't let her come to any harm."

It was Bill Trent who asked, "Now how can you do that? Are you going to hide out in the Everglades again?"

"Someplace better. We'll stay aboard the *Atlantis*. Go south to the Keys, take a little trip into the Gulf of Mexico, maybe." His voice had been dreamy, now it hardened. "But you've got to catch those killers, Bill. You have to promise me that."

"I'm going to pay a visit to Dolly Donati. I'm going to throw the fear of God into him." He eyed Kai a moment, then added, "I'd appreciate it if you'd come with me, Miss Pierce."

"Hey," Rod snapped. "She's in danger."

The police lieutenant shook his head. "Oh, no. Not if she's with me. And with her brother. You too, I guess. I want Kai to confront him; I want to learn why he wants her dead."

Kai felt terror touch her for a moment. Yet Rod was reaching to grip her hand, pressing it. "Only if we go armed," Rod said. "I carry a gun, so does Ken. I'm not taking any chances."

Trent smiled. "Okay, okay. You can carry guns. But Dolly will be insulted. He doesn't shoot guests." He rubbed his jaw thoughtfully. "As a matter of fact, I'm surprised that Dolly had his boys shooting at Kai. It isn't like him, not at all. Sure, sure, he's a gangster, but until now he's always been a polite one."

Kai looked down at herself. "I can't go like this! I have to change my clothes."

"I brought along the clothes I bought for you," Rod murmured. "But they're not the sort of thing you should wear. No, it should be something breathtaking, something—ha! Got it. We'll go shopping."

Kai frowned. "I have my Enza, that I didn't wear to dinner the night you kidnapped me."

The police lieutenant looked interested. "Kidnapped?"

Kai gave him a dazzling smile. "That's what I call it. Actually, Ken and Rod agreed that I should disappear, right after that attack on me. So they pretended it was a kidnapping. Actually, I went along of my own free will."

Rod gave her hand a squeeze, then said, "Kai and I are driving up to Palm Beach to buy her something to wear. Ken, you stay with Sandra."

Ken seemed pleased by that idea, Kai noted. He said, "I'd better go up and keep her company. It can get pretty lonesome on that bridge."

Her brother had never thought it was lonely for *her*, Kai told herself. Yet she was glad to see him clamber up the ladder. It would keep Sandra away from Rod.

The big cruiser slid through the waves, its twin diesels humming softly. The decks were clean, the brassworks highly polished. Paint glistened everywhere Kai looked. Even the cushions on which they were sitting seemed brand new. She didn't know how much a small yacht like this would cost, but it must have been plenty. Obviously, Rod could not have afforded it on his income as a professor.

That meant that he had inherited money, most probably. Or else those books he had written had brought him in a small fortune. It would be fun to take a cruise on the *Atlantis*, just herself and Rod. She thought about that, sitting there and dreaming as Rod and the police lieutenant chatted.

Rod caught hold of her hand, smiling down at her, "Come on, Kai. We have to feed our guests."

"*Our* guests?"

"Sure, ours. You're the lady of the *Atlantis*, now. We must be hospitable."

Pleasure ran all through her. How wonderful it would be if she really were the lady of this cruiser! Of course, that would mean she would have to marry Rod. To her vast surprise, that idea did not seem as impossible as it had a few days ago.

Remembering how she had hated Rod when she had first seen him climbing out of the ocean—after she had thought he'd attacked her!—Kai giggled. How wrong could a girl be? Now all she felt toward him was tenderness and—yes, possessiveness. The mere idea of Sandra getting Rod was enough to make her see red.

"What's so funny?" Rod wondered.

Kai shook her head. "Girl secrets. Things you aren't supposed to know."

"Nice things?"

He had halted her on the threshold of the galley, turning her so that he was staring into her eyes. Those blue eyes of his were informing her that he thought her the most beautiful girl in the entire world, and that he wanted her as his own, very much.

"What sort of nice things?" he asked softly. "Does that mean what I hope it does?"

She smiled happily. "Could be. Oh, now—no, don't. Rod, we——"

He ignored her words to catch her in his arms, to hold her and kiss her. The touch of his lips on hers made her cling to him for support. She was not able to think, all she could do was hang on and let him feast his mouth on hers as much as he wanted. Of course, she was feasting on his lips, as well.

A vague little voice somewhere inside her head told Kai that if she were to go on this cruise with him to avoid getting killed by those gangsters—and she was going, all right!—she would have to watch her step. There would have to be no more kissing and hugging.

Baloney! If he didn't grab and kiss you, you'd hate him!

She pressed closer, holding him tightly.

Somebody from the deck said, "This sea air does give one an appetite, doesn't it?"

She broke away from Rod guiltily, still clinging to him,

but laughing softly. "We're a fine example of host and hostess. Here we are pleasing ourselves and we have guests starving to death outside."

Rod sighed. "Duty first, I guess."

They went into the galley, removing cut meats from the refrigerator and bread from the breadbox. Rod made coffee as Kai built sandwiches. We work well together, she was thinking, we seem to act together as if we were doing it for years. Rod was humming softly to himself and Kai realized that she was happier than she had ever been in her life.

"Come and get it," Rod yelled.

He went out then, to put the *Atlantis* on automatic so that Sandra and Ken could sit down and eat. A glance out the galley porthole told Kai that they were alone out on the ocean, that the cruiser could run by itself for a time without worry.

Sandra seemed almost to have forgotten Rod's existence, Kai was pleased to see. She was devoting her attention to Ken, listening to him explain how he and Kai had been searching for the wrecked *Santa Maria Gloriosa* for the past two years.

"Kai found some old records in a library in Mexico City that related how a treasure fleet had set out from Cartagena back in the seventeenth century and had been separated by a storm. Some of the ships survived that hurricane, but the *Santa Maria Gloriosa* was driven off course and wrecked somewhere off the coast of Florida."

Sandra frowned slightly. "That isn't much help. Florida has an awfully long coastline."

"True. But we've done a lot of calculating. We know in what direction that hurricane was blowing. There are only a few places where the *Gloriosa* could be."

"Sounds like hunting for a needle in the proverbial haystack to me," Bill Trent offered.

Ken smiled wanly. "We've discovered that, we haven't had any success at all. But we aren't giving up. The money's down there—millions of dollars in gold bars and uncut jewels. Whoever finds it is going to be mighty rich."

Sandra wriggled excitedly. "Oooooh, it sounds like fun.

Could I come along and help you look? I'm an expert diver."

"You sure can," Ken nodded, smiling at her.

"Not, however," the police lieutenant said slowly, "until we solve the riddle of who it is who wants to kill Kai."

Sandra glanced at Kai. "Whoever wants to kill her wouldn't want to kill me. I doubt that anyone would mistake me for her."

"Well, I'm not exactly convinced that it's only Kai whose life is in danger."

Everyone looked at Trent. He gestured, scowling slightly, saying, "Look, it may be that whoever tried to kill her wanted to prevent her from finding something down there on the bottom. Or if she's already found it, to prevent her from talking about it."

Kai stared at him. "What in the world can that be?"

Trent shrugged. "I just don't know. That's why I don't want any of you doing any diving around that same spot. Not until we solve this matter."

Rod sipped the last of his coffee. "I have to go up to the wheelhouse. You stay here and talk all you want."

Kai rose, saying, "I'll do the dishes. You others go out on deck and enjoy the air." She looked at Rod. "I'll be done shortly, and come and join you."

Sandra remained behind to dry the dishes. As she helped Kai clear the table, she asked, "Do you and your brother really expect to find that treasure?"

"We hope to. If we don't, we've wasted a lot of time."

They worked in silence for a time, then Sandra said, "I've always felt that looking for sunken treasure was a big waste of time. Until now, that is."

Kai looked at her, placing a wet dish on the drainboard. "Oh? And now?"

"I'd like to help," the other girl said slowly. "Oh, I don't mean I'd want any of the treasure—except maybe for a jewel I'd have made into a ring for the fun of it. No, it would just be for the fun of it."

There was a wistfulness in her voice that touched Kai. She washed the last dish and reached for a towel. As she was drying her hands, she murmured, "Why don't you speak to Ken about it? I'll be gone for a time, with Rod."

She waited for some reaction from Sandra, but the golden goddess only nodded. "Maybe you and he could go diving, as he and I have been doing. But not for a while. I really don't feel it would be safe."

Sandra eyed her closely. "Somebody really did try to kill you, then?"

"Of course. Maybe he did me a favor, though. If he hadn't tried to kill me, I'd never have met Rod."

Sandra smiled. "You like him, don't you?"

Kai wondered how much she could admit. "Yes, I like him."

The golden goddess shrugged. "I wish you luck. I haven't had any. It's as if Rod were insulated against women."

Kai grinned, remembering the hugs and kisses. Then she felt sorry for Sandra. The girl was beautiful, she was rich, and Kai began to sense that she was desperately unhappy.

She said slyly, "Ken hasn't had much to do with girls, either. But I don't think he's insulated against them. He's been too busy hunting for treasure to get himself involved."

Sandra's eyes brightened. "I like him," she said slowly, and her eyes asked a question of Kai.

"If you really do, then go after him." Kai smiled. "He'll be lonely right now, with me gone off with Rod."

The golden goddess hugged her. "I'll do it. Come on!"

They went out on deck together, Sandra making a beeline toward Ken where he sat with the police lieutenant, Kai climbing the ladder to the wheelhouse. She sat down on the aft seat, directly behind Rod, who turned and smiled at her.

"We'll be in port in another hour," he told her. "Then we're going shopping, to get you a new dress."

"No, we're not. I have enough clothes. Besides, I don't want you wasting your money."

"Oh? But I want to buy you things."

"Some other time, then. But not now. My Enza is good enough to go see that gangster. After that—well, I won't need fancy clothes on the *Atlantis*, will I?"

"Just a couple of bathing suits."

They came into the harbor in the late afternoon, with Bill Trent insisting that they go at once to visit Dolly Donati. "There's no time like the present. Besides, a couple of those hoods might be with Dolly. If they are, I'm hoping they'll start something."

Rod drove them all to the little Pierce house where Ken made coffee while Kai fled into her tiny bedroom to change into the Enka. She was a little frightened, she admitted as she stared at her reflection in the mirror. She had never seen a gangster before, to her knowledge. If this Dolly Donati was the killer Bill Trent thought him to be, he might order them all shot down.

Still, she found Rod very supportive as she sat beside him in the Continental.

"Just look scared," he told her, squeezing her hand.

"I can do that easily enough. I am scared."

"And let Bill do the talking. He's used to this sort of thing."

In a small voice, she asked, "Do you really have a gun on you?"

"Sure, in my back pocket. A Mauser automatic. I usually keep it on the *Atlantis* in my cabin."

She stared at him. "Why would you need a gun on the *Atlantis*?"

"No special reason. Sometimes when I'm off on the ocean I'll throw a tin can or a bottle into the water and practice my marksmanship on it."

"Do you ever hit it?"

"Sometimes. After about half a dozen shots. I'm a lot better with a rifle."

"Let's hope you'll never have to use it."

"When we go off by ourselves, you can shoot with it, too."

Kai shivered. "Not me. I'm afraid of firearms."

Rod turned in at a big iron gate, braking the car. The police car pulled in beside him. Kai watched Bill Trent get out and move toward the gatehouse, where he was met by the gatekeeper. They talked for a few minutes, then the gatekeeper went inside the gatehouse where he picked up a phone.

In moments, they were moving up a graveled driveway

toward a huge mansion. Crime must surely pay, Kai thought as she studied the big house. It was of gray granite, with lighted windows on the first floor, with a big garage to the rear.

Kai moved up the steps between Rod and Ken, with Sandra on Ken's other side. The door opened and a man stood there, bulking huge and muscular in a gray sweater. His eyes, hooded and wary, took them all in.

"The boss says to show you right in," he muttered. Then to Bill Trent he nodded his head. "Hiya, lieutenant."

Trent grinned. "Good to see you, Mike. Keeping your nose clean?"

"Aw, come on, lieutenant. I been a good boy lately."

Gray Sweater walked ahead of them, opening a door and then standing back to let them enter. Kai saw a large room, oak-paneled, with bookshelves crammed with books along two walls, and a magnificent oak desk behind which sat a small lean man with a hard face.

"Hi, Dolly," said Trent.

Dolly Donati stood, coming around the edge of the desk with his hand out. As they shook hands, the gangster asked Trent, "Now, what's this all about?"

"First let me introduce everyone, Dolly." When the introductions were made, the lieutenant gestured at Kai. "Your boys have been trying to kill this young lady, Dolly. What I want to know is—why?"

Donati turned and eyed Kai. His eyes were cold, hard, but they softened as they regarded her. He shook his head. "Must be some mistake, lieutenant. My boys don't go around shooting pretty girls."

"Tell him, Kai."

Kai began to talk. As she did, Donati's eyes got wider and wider. Something like disbelief flickered across his face, but that disbelief changed slowly as she went on talking. When she was done, Dolly Donati gestured to them all.

"Sit down, sit down. We got to talk about this." When he was seated behind his desk, he leaned forward to put his elbows on it, turning to look at Bill Trent.

"You got this all wrong. My boys didn't try to kill her."

"It was your cruiser out there. I recognized it."

The gangster shook his head. "No, it wasn't. I got rid of that boat a few months ago. Bought myself another one. Bigger and better. The question seems to be, who bought my old one?"

"Assuming you're telling the truth, why should the purchaser of your old yacht want to kill Kai?"

Donati turned his head and eyed Kai. "I can't guess, lieutenant. The guy must be nuts." He turned back to Trent. "I'll put my boys on it. I'll have them ask around."

"Do that. I'll be asking, myself."

"One more thing, lieutenant," the gangster said slowly. "Somebody is trying to muscle in on me."

Bill Trent shrugged. "What do you want me to do about it?"

"I've lost half a dozen boys. What I want you to do is—find their bodies!"

"Hold on. Give that to me again, carefully."

Donati hunched forward on the table. "There's been a gang war going on. I didn't know about it until a day or two ago—I've been away. Now I find that six or seven of my boys are missing. Presumed dead. The trouble is, there's no proof of that. I can't find their bodies. And believe me, I've hunted for them."

Bill Trent sat back in his chair, staring at Donati. "Are you telling me what I think you are? Someone's shooting your mobsters, and you can't find their bodies?"

A cold smile flickered across Dolly Donati's face. "Got it first crack, lieutenant. Can you help?"

"I'll ask around. I'm not promising anything, but I will make inquiries. First off, I'll ask you: Who profits by their deaths?"

"I don't know. Somebody, for sure. Another mob, maybe, planning to take over my territory."

Trent asked softly, "You have no idea who that might be?"

"No idea. None at all. My second in command—you know Barf Cignalia—has been asking around, too. He hasn't come up with anything."

Kai was studying the police lieutenant. He was smiling almost happily, there was humor in his eyes at which she was surprised, because what they had been talking about was far from funny. He shifted forward on his easychair and shook a finger at the gangster.

"Dolly, come off it. You can try to fool these people with me, and maybe that's why you're clamming up. But I know better and you know better. Does the name Cheeks Tegrino mean anything to you?"

Kai saw Donati's hand quiver a moment, but his face was the same deadpan it always was. Then his eyebrows rose slightly.

"Cheeks Tegrino?"

"Sure. He comes from Detroit. You and he had an argument about three, four years ago."

"Oh. *That* Cheeks Tegrino. Yeah, I know him."

"He's been seen in and around Miami."

Donati looked at Kai, at her brother, at Sandra Alberts, and at Rod Grant. Just a brushing with his eyes, but Kai would have sworn that he knew all about them. He shrugged, and leaned back in his chair. A smile touched his thin lips. Then he spread his hands.

"So okay. You want me to level with you. So I'll level. The bastard is here in Florida with some of his boys."

"Go on," Trent prodded.

"I can't prove a thing."

"Then let me do the talking. Somebody's been killing your boys. But you can't prove who's doing it."

Something broke in Dolly Donati. His voice became a snarl. "Sure, I know that. Those boys wouldn't disappear on me. No way. So somebody's been rubbing them out. But—I can't prove anything."

The police lieutenant sighed. "Neither can I, unfortunately. But I'm working on it." He glanced at Kai. "I didn't think you or your men were after Kai there. But I wanted to be sure."

"I don't go around shooting women!"

"I know that. What I want to know is—would Tegrino?"

Donati stiffened. His eyes glazed over and coldness

seemed to exude from him. His eyes grew thoughtful. For a moment, there was absolute stillness in the room.

"He might, though he's never done it before, to my knowledge. I hate his guts, but I got to say I'd be surprised if he did."

Trent's voice was very soft. "Might he shoot at Kai here—as a warning? Not to hit her, but to scare her off?"

Kai sat upright, her eyes going to one man and then the other. "Scare me off?" she repeated.

Neither man glanced at her. Their eyes were locked, they went on staring at each other. Slowly, Dolly Donati nodded, almost whispering. "Yeah. He might. If he had something to hide."

"The treasure!" Kai yelped. "He's found the *Santa Maria Gloriosa* and he doesn't want anybody else finding it!"

Dolly Donati turned and eyed her. For a moment, he seemed about to speak, but Bill Trent forestalled him.

"That's what I think, too," he said. "He's found the gold and the jewels and he means to have them for his own."

The gangster scowled. "But——"

Trent's sudden gesture kept him silent. It was as if some unspoken message ran between one man and the other. They were a conflict in ideals, in beliefs, in what each man stood for, yet there seemed to be an understanding between them, almost a joining of interests.

The police lieutenant stood. "You keep your nose clean, Dolly. You and I have always gotten along, more or less. You let me handle this."

"What about my boys?" Donati asked hoarsely. "You think I'm going to sit back and let them get shot or whatever happened to them, and not do anything?"

"Sure I do. I don't want a gang war in my territory. I'll handle this. I'm giving it top priority. I'm pulling all the strings I can, I'm going to have everybody who can be spared in the department working on it. I don't want you cutting in, or somebody will get hurt."

Donati looked at him for several moments. His shoulders lifted and fell. "So okay. I'll hold back. I won't do anything—yet."

They shook hands. At a gesture from Trent, the others got to their feet and turned toward the door. As she was going out, Kai gave Dolly Donati a glance over her shoulder. The little man was standing behind his desk, staring down at it, and he was gnawing on his lower lip. He seemed very worried.

Out in the air, Rod asked Bill Trent, "Will he do as you ask? Will he keep his men back?"

"For a time. But I've got to get busy, I've got to keep an eye on Tegrino and his boys. I want to let them know that they're under suspicion. Oh, I have ways to do that. What I have to do now is to stop whoever it is from murdering any more of Dolly's crowd."

Rod nodded. "While you're doing all that, Kai and I will disappear."

Sandra leaned past Ken's shoulder to ask, "Where?"

Rod grinned. "We're taking off on the *Atlantis* for a week or two." He glanced at Trent. "Will that be long enough?"

"I think so."

Sandra said, "If those men don't want to kill Kai, just scare her as that man said, there's no need to run away by yourselves."

Kai could have murdered her cheerfully. She held her breath, waiting for Rod to say something. She could have kissed him when he said, "But we don't know that. We aren't taking any chances."

That was when Ken murmured, "Time will drag a little heavily on my hands without you, Kai. I won't know what to do with myself."

Sandra looked up at him, smiling. "I could help pass the time for you," she offered.

"Lady, that was what I wanted to hear. Now I suggest that we all go find a place to eat. I'm starving."

"You run ahead without me," Bill Trent suggested. "I have to get working on this matter."

Three hours later, they stood on the dock to which the *Atlantis* was moored, saying their farewells. Kai had packed a small bag containing a couple of bathing suits, a nightgown and a pair of pyjamas she had never yet worn, together with her makeup kit, a comb and brush. She was excited, yet nervous at the same time.

She had never done anything like this, going off alone with a man. Well, never except for those days she had spent in the Everglades with Rod. But that wasn't quite the same thing. She had been kidnapped then—or almost. She was a little fearful.

Oh, not of Rod. She could handle him, all right. It was herself that she was frightened of, because she knew very well that where Rod was concerned, she was definitely not the Kai Pierce she had always been. Oh my, no. She seemed an entirely different girl.

If he so much as touched her, chills went up and down her spine. She turned to mush inside when those blue eyes of his fastened on her. She had to be very careful of him during this next week or two. Stay clear of him, don't give him a chance to put those arms of his around her.

That way led to surrender.

Her heart began to bang, thinking about surrendering to Rod Grant. To be held in those muscular arms, to be kissed and hugged and touched here and there by his powerful—yet gentle—hands, was something she longed for.

Hey! Cut out thinking like that! Remember, she had to stay clear of him. Yet her body remembered the touch of his when he held her tightly, her lips ached to be kissed to breathlessness. Ha! If she went on thinking like this, and feeling these emotions, she would collapse if he so much as held her hand.

"You all right?" a voice asked.

Kai blinked. "I—I'm sorry. What was that?"

Ken grinned. "Sandra and I are leaving. Say good-bye for a little while, Kai."

"Oh! Oh, yes. Of course. So long, Ken. Bye, Sandra— and take good care of my brother."

"I will, I will," Sandra sang.

Then Rod was gripping her arm, helping her aboard the *Atlantis,* then moving to throw off the ropes that held the cruiser to the dock. Kai watched him, admiring his big body, its grace and ease of movement. As he came back along the side deck, she shook herself and stepped to meet him.

"What must you think of me?" she asked. "I've been lost in daydreams! Tell me what you want me to do."

"Not a thing. I'm going up to the wheelhouse now and get underway. You care to lie down? Or go to bed?"

"Already? With a moon like that up there in the sky? Certainly not."

"Come along, then. We can talk as I take her out into the ocean."

She preceded him up the ladder, relishing the quiet of the night, the soft plash-plash of the waves striking the beach off to one side. Something inside her was singing happily, yet there was a tiny part of her trying to tell her to be careful.

"You have beautiful legs," Rod was saying.

It came to her that she was wearing the Enka dress and not slacks. Oh my God! If he were staring at her under her skirt. . . .

She stepped onto the wheelhouse floor, using her hands, now that they were free, to pull her skirt against her. She felt her cheeks flushing in the nighttime darkness. But even as she felt indignation, it seemed to ebb out of her.

"You shouldn't have," she scolded.

He was beside her, now, smiling down at her. "Why not? I love you. I love all of you, your legs included. So why shouldn't I tell you that your legs are gorgeous? They are."

Rod hesitated, then asked, "Are you trying to imply that you have lousy legs?"

Kai gaped at him. "Lousy legs? Certainly not!"

"Then what's the difference if I admire them? Besides, they're going to be mine some day."

Kai stuttered, trying to find words. But Rod had gone to the controls and was pressing buttons, starting the big diesels. He seemed almost to have forgotten her. But he was not going to forget her. Oh, no!

She walked up to him where he was standing, the wheel in his hands, as the *Atlantis* began surging forward.

"What did you mean by that? Saying that my legs are going to belong to you?"

"All of you is. Don't your legs go along with all of you?"

"I am not going to belong to you."

"Sure you are. I've made up my mind."

Kai wished her heart would stop banging away. It seemed to act independently of whatever she was doing or saying. Right now she was snapping, "Oh, have you? And what about my mind?"

"That, too. It all comes in the same package."

Kai tossed her head. "I do *not* belong to you!"

"Right. Not now. But soon."

He was most annoying, Kai told herself. Especially when he turned his face toward her and she could see his eyes just about eating at her. Those blue eyes did certain things to her body that puzzled her.

"I will never belong to you," she stated coldly.

"When we get married, you will. Just as I'll belong to you."

He said it so quietly that it took a moment for his words to sink in. Then she snapped, "I will not marry you!"

Rod turned and caught her, bringing her body in against his, covering her mouth with his lips. Oh, damn! She should never have stood so close to him! It was almost like inviting him to do what he was doing. . . .

"Silly little goose," he whispered against her mouth, after several moments. "Don't you know I'm heels over head in love with you? That I adore you? That I want you beside me all the rest of my life?"

He kissed her again, before she could say anything.

She wished he wouldn't hold her so tightly. No, she didn't. It was glorious to be gripped and kissed this way. She had never known anything like it. Yet she had to object, or all he would be doing during the next week or two would be making love to her.

"You have to stop," she panted.

"You're right. The ship needs steering. We can't be riding all over the ocean, can we?"

Why not? The heck with the ocean!

Yet she stepped back, curiously shy. Rod caught her, moved her to stand behind the wheel. "You steer. It's better that way."

Kai found herself with the wheel in her hands, easing the *Atlantis* through the long lift and fall of the ocean waves. Rod was off to one side, doing something—she didn't know what, she didn't dare look for fear he would grab her again—and she told herself that if that happened, there wouldn't be any stopping him.

She would not be able to stop him, that was for sure. Her legs were still trembling, her middle was still mushy, from what had happened seconds ago. She had to get a grip on herself, on her strength, on her nerves. Somehow, she had to find the old Kai Pierce, the one who scorned all men.

Kai had to find that lost part of her psyche! Revitalize it, so that the next time Rod should grab her, she could fight him off instead of yielding so spinelessly. It was imperative.

Who are you kidding? He said he wanted to marry you!
"No," she breathed.

She was afraid of marriage. Always, she had been her own individual: independent, self-sufficient. If she should marry Rod—not that there was the slightest chance of that, but—just suppose. Why, she would lose everything she held dearest! No more independence. No more doing her own thing.

Kai scowled. What *was* her own thing? Swimming along the ocean bottom hunting for a treasure that was never there? Never where it ought to be? What kind of a life was that, anyhow?

She brooded, staring ahead through the wheelhouse glass. Only after a time did she realize that there were tears in her eyes.

Eight

Two DAYS LATER, the *Atlantis* was a few miles south of Sands Key, east of Elliott Key. Its prow clove through the surging waves, lifting and falling, driving steadily southward. The sun shone down in all its brightness, baking Kai where she lay sunbathing on the forward deck, out of sight of Rod behind the wheel.

Kai was not happy. Well, she told herself, she was not unhappy. Not exactly, that is. The whole trouble was Roderick Grant. He was playing the part of gentleman to perfection.

After that first night, when they had left Boca Raton, he hadn't so much as grabbed her, let alone kissed her. It was as if he had made a commitment to himself, that he would not show any sign of affection toward her. Any physical sign, that is.

Oh, he stared at her enough, eating her with his eyes, devouring her. She admitted that, with a pleasant shiver. It was as though his blue eyes were promising to make mad, wild love to her—just as soon as they were married. Kai stabbed out at empty air with her foot. Why did the big jerk have to be so noble? Sure. Sure. She had told him not to hug and kiss her. But why did he have to believe her?

Didn't he realize that a girl said things she didn't really mean to the man she loved? Of course, Rod didn't realize she loved him. How could he? She herself hadn't realized it until very recently. But that didn't excuse him. What sort of man was he, anyhow?

A gentleman. Ha! Kai sneered.

Even this skimpy two-piece bathing suit—what there was of it, that is—apparently had no effect on him. Hmmm. He did look. She gave him that. His eyes all but ate her up, sending little chills and thrills all over her when she caught him doing it.

But what fun was that? It was as though he was teasing her, and Kai had never been one to enjoy teasing. Why couldn't he just have grabbed her, held her tightly, and then smothered her with kisses? She would have put up a struggle, though a very weak one, just enough to let him understand that when he did overcome her, their lovemaking would be all the more enjoyable.

"You asleep?"

Kai opened one eye. Rod was standing there in his swim briefs, very tanned, very muscular, rather handsome. He was smiling gently at her, even as his eyes were caressing her exposed flesh. There was a lot of her flesh to be caressed, too, in the tiny things she had on.

"Just dozing," she replied.

"You've cooked enough. How about a swim?"

"You go. I'm too comfortable."

She wanted him to reach down, drag her to her feet, put his arms around her, and kiss her. After they had kissed and hugged enough, they could dive into the ocean and cool off.

"Okay, then. Be seeing you."

Kai sat up just in time to watch him step to the edge of the cruiser and dive off. She gritted her teeth, sat up, and hooked both arms about her legs.

"Dope! Stupid! Ignoramus!" she breathed.

She would make him suffer for this cavalier treatment of her. Just how, she did not know. She could hardly refuse him her favors when he didn't seem at all interested in those favors. Kai scowled darkly. There had to be a way.

Her eyes went to where Rod was swimming easily through the waves, making good time. He was an excellent swimmer, she admitted, he was like a porpoise in the ocean. Her eyes slid to the waves, and she shivered.

Ever since that near escape of hers, she had dreaded going into the water. Well, that was understandable. Still! She had to overcome that fear if she were going to be around Rod very much. As she was, for the next ten or twelve days.

The *Atlantis* was drifting slowly, alone on the Atlantic as far as she could tell. There wasn't another boat in sight. It was a gorgeous day, with the sun a hot golden ball up in a cloudless sky. A perfect day for swimming, for laughing, for fooling around with the man she loved.

"Oh, phooey!"

She was going to have to do something about it. For sure, Rod wasn't going to. He must actually believe that she wanted him to stay at arm's length. Somehow—without being too obvious, naturally—she must disabuse him of that notion. She began to grin.

Rising to her feet, she went to get a towel. Rod was coming back to the boat, swimming strongly. Getting rid of his excess energy, no doubt.

"I can think of better ways of getting rid of it," she muttered to herself.

Then Rod was coming up the side, rising to the deck, swinging onto it. As he did, Kai was there beside him with the towel, putting it on him, rubbing him with it, drying him off. His surprised look made her want to giggle, but she fought down her mirth.

"Can't have you catching cold," she told him, rubbing away.

"I really don't think you'd better," he told her.

"If you get sick, what will happen? Just be a good boy and let me take care of you."

"That's the trouble."

"What's the trouble?"

"I can't go on being a good boy with you toweling me off like this."

Her eyes opened wide, filled with innocence. "Why ever not?"

"I can't go on being a good boy. You're too near."

"So? What difference does that make?"

His hands caught her, jammed her up against his almost naked body. Oh, my! She had forgotten what the touching of their bodies did to her! She lay against him, head tilted backward so she could stare up into his eyes.

"It makes this difference," he breathed. "I want you, silly. I want you more than I can possibly tell you. I've been behaving myself. I can't go on behaving myself."

His kiss electrified her. She tingled to the tips of her toes that were curling slightly as though with high voltage shock. Her middle absolutely melted, and her legs were like limp rags. She clung to him for support.

When their kiss ended, she hung on to him, her face against his hairy chest. Woweee! Her head was reeling, she had no more strength in her than in a baby kitten. Dope that she was, she had not remembered what his kisses did to her.

"Let me go," she whispered pleadingly.

"Oh, no. I like it like this—and so do you."

"I do not!"

His voice was teasing. "Oh, yes, you do. You're a sweet little fraud, Kai Pierce. A lovely, darling faker. You love me, but you won't admit it."

She shook her head back and forth, against his chest.

"If it weren't for your brother. . . ."

Ah. That made her jerk her head up and stare into his blue eyes, eyes that seemed to swallow her up. Weakly, she asked, "What's my brother got to do with us?"

"I made him an implied promise that I would take care of you. How would it look to him if I made love to you when I was supposed to be protecting you?"

Phooey on her brother!

"Did you?" she wanted to know. "Did you actually promise him?"

"Not in so many words, no."

She pushed him away, almost angrily. "If my brother means so much to you, then keep your promise!"

Kai walked away, as far as she could go. But Rod

came after her, catching her by the arm and swinging her back to him.

"Don't be angry," he whispered.

"I will so be angry if I want to be! I thought you were a man."

His arms closed around her, lifting her off her feet. He was so strong! Kai could hardly even wriggle. And when she did wriggle, up against him like this, it did strange things to her.

There was laughter in his voice as he murmured, "A man, is it? So you don't think I'm a man. Well, now. . . ."

He was inching his way closer to the edge of the deck. An appalling thought came to Kai. "Don't you dare!" she yelled.

Too late! He was overbalancing them, falling overside. Kai yelled and automatically clung to him as they went down together into the ocean. Down into greenish depths they went, before Rod began to swim upward with her. Only when they reached the surface did he release his hold on her.

Kai spluttered, "You meanie!"

"It was either this or carry you into my cabin."

She glanced at him. She was not really angry, Kai realized. The cold water was invigorating, it made her feel fully, vitally alive. What was that he had said? Either dunk her this way or carry her into his cabin. So why was she wet?

Maybe the chilliness of the water was putting some sense into her. It was better this way, far better. If he had taken her into his cabin, there was no telling what might have happened.

Well, now that she was in the ocean, she might as well swim. She struck out, moving vigorously, aware that Rod was keeping up with her very easily. Kai unleashed a burst of speed, but could not lose him. Her brother had been right. Rod was an excellent swimmer.

She turned, after a time, to swim back to the boat. She was having a good time, she realized. It was fun, racing Rod this way, using her muscles, feeling life surge through her so strongly. It had been some time since she had felt so filled with energy.

Part of this well-being, she knew, was because it was Rod who swam beside her. Now that in itself was strange. All her life, she had depended on no one but herself. In a way, it annoyed her that she seemed to be depending on Rod for this feeling that surged through her so strongly.

As she clung to the boat's ladder, Rod was there to lend her a hand to climb it. For an instant, she considered telling him she could climb these rungs by herself, but the touch of his hand to her arm changed her mind.

She caught the ladder, bent to put a foot on it. Rod's hands moved down to her haunches, lifted her up. His arms and hands were very strong, they buoyed her up, raising her so easily that she was halfway up the ladder before she realized it.

As she stepped onto the deck, he swung up beside her.

"There, you see?" he was saying. "You weren't afraid any more."

"Afraid?"

"Sure, afraid. Don't think I don't know how reluctant you are to go into the water. Mind, I don't blame you. But if we're going to get married———"

"We are *not* going to get married!"

His gesture brushed aside her words. "When we get married, we'll do a lot of boating and swimming. You love it—or used to. I want you to love it just as I do."

Kai glowered at him. How could she get it through his thick skull that she was not going to marry him? Words didn't seem to impress him, not at all. Come to think of it, even her own words to herself didn't seem to impress her, either.

Now why was that?

Kai walked toward where her big beach towel was spread on the deck. Bending, she lifted it, began rubbing herself dry.

"Hey, let me do that," he urged, reaching for the towel.

"Don't you dare."

"I can reach those hard-to-get-at places."

She gave him a sharp glance, discovered that he was

grinning all over his face. Irritated, she snapped, "You just want to get your hands on me."

"Of course I do. And you want me to. Deep down, you do. But you're scared."

"I've never been scared of anything in my life."

"That's what helps make you so lovable."

"I am not lovable," she grated.

"I think you are. I think you're the most lovable woman in the entire world. You're so beautiful, Kai! So—so magnificent! I only wish you could see yourself as I see you. Then you'd realize that God created you just for me to adore and worship."

She stared up at him, fully aware of the fact that she was getting all mushy again, inside herself. When he talked like that, she was just about ready to roll over and play dead for him.

Hmmm. Well, maybe not dead. Oh, no. If he would reach out and grab her, she would become very much alive. Maybe for the first time in her life. The new life that swim had put into her would be as nothing compared to it.

Hey, girl. Stop thinking like that. You know what it might lead to.

Rod reached out and put his hand on the small of her back. His touch was akin to an electric shock, only much more pleasant. Much more! He ran his palm up and down.

"A little wet spot you missed," he murmured.

"Oh?" she asked in a small voice.

His hand moved caressingly. "No need to give me the towel. I can dry it this way."

She had not been about to hand him the fluffy beach cloth. As a matter of fact, she had not been about to do anything except stand here and let delightful chills run up and down her spine from his touch.

Only when the radius of his rubbing grew larger—he was stroking her hip at the moment—did she stir restlessly. "You'd better stop," she murmured.

His voice was dreamy as he asked, "Why? I like it."

"So do I. And I don't want to."

"You're being very silly," he went on in that languorous voice. "It isn't very often in our lives that we human beings find something that we enjoy. Really enjoy, I mean. This is one of those times."

Almost imperceptibly, his strokings were bringing her closer, ever closer. Her thigh touched his, her hip was pressing into him. Really! She ought to pull away. Her legs were getting weaker, ever weaker. Fortunately, she could not move.

His arm was hooking her slim waist, now. He had forgotten about that damp spot, he was unashamedly caressing her. And Kai loved it. A part of her wanted him to go on doing what he was doing, even to extending his field of operations. Ah, but she knew there would be no stopping him if he did. Or stopping herself, for that matter.

"You promised my brother," she made herself say.

Instantly, his hand fell away and Kai cursed under her breath. What was the matter with her? Here she was on the very edge of heaven, and she had to go and open her big mouth. Just a few more minutes and he would have been kissing her, and neither she nor he would have been able to stop when that happened.

Not the way she was feeling. Not the way he was, either.

His face was flushed, even under the tan. His blue eyes were feeding on her eyes, telling them how very much he needed her. Her eyes were probably doing the same thing, she knew.

Somebody had to be strong.

"I'd better go for another swim," he muttered.

Kai smiled wryly. "We can't be forever jumping in and out of the ocean."

"True. But I have to—ah—calm down."

"What makes you think I don't?"

His hand caught hers and tugged. Kai sighed and dropped the towel. Rod was right. They both needed a cooling off. She ran with him to the edge and dove.

The water closed around them and they swam side by side for a time. Then they turned back and raced to the boat. Rod was there when Kai reached out to grip the lower rung of the ladder. She shook water from her hair and eyed him.

"Cooled off?" she giggled.

"For a time," he laughed.

"You go up first, this time. It's safer."

He went up the ladder, agile as a monkey. Then he reached a hand down to grip her wrist and swing her up beside him. They stood there looking at each other, water dripping from them onto the deck.

"I'll dry off by sunbathing," she offered.

"Good idea! I'll join you, but at a distance."

They lay down together on the deck, at a reasonably safe distance. Kai closed her eyes, took a deep breath of the salt ocean air. She had to be sensible, she assured herself. In cases such as this, it is always the woman who must be strong. A man was weak where it came to denying himself the pleasures of the flesh.

She asked, "What do you want for lunch?"

"You."

There was so much hunger in his voice that she shivered. She made herself say, "Come on. Be sensible. Something to eat."

"Your little finger."

"Aside from that."

"Okay, then. One of your toes. Cute little toes. I love them."

"I need my toes. And my little finger, too."

"Oh, I wouldn't eat it all. I'd just nibble a little."

She was smiling, lying there on her back with the hot Florida sun beating down on her all but naked body. It would be fun to have Rod nibble at her finger. Or even her toe. But then he would want to nibble at other things, too, and Kai was fully aware that she might not be able to stop him. Might not want to, either.

"We have to be sensible," she whispered.

His sigh was heavy. "I know, I know. You know what the trouble is? We don't have any destination."

"What sort of destination?"

"Some place to go. Something to do. Something to occupy our time. For instance, I know a place in Coral Gables that serves steaks so tender they melt in your mouth. Berry pie, too—maybe with ice cream on it. There's only one thing wrong with something like that."

"What could be wrong with it?"

"A meal like that would give me too much energy."

Kai giggled. "You have to be strong, Rod. As strong-willed as you are strong-bodied."

Rod groaned. Then he said, "How about it? Do we make for Coral Gables?"

"We might as well."

Rod rose up and moved around to the wheelhouse. Moments later, Kai could hear the throbbing of the twin diesels. The *Atlantis* surged forward, sliding through the waves. Kai stretched, relishing the bite of the sun, the soft caress of the sea wind. It was so pleasant, so relaxing, that she almost dreaded getting up and putting on clothes.

She turned over and lay on her stomach, snuggling her head in her arms. There was plenty of time to put something on. She dozed.

It was hours later that they came in sight of the shore. Kai stood beside Rod in the wheelhouse, clad in the Enka dress. Rod had put on slacks and a turtle-necked pullover. He looked brawny and extremely healthy—maybe almost too healthy—and Kai found herself feasting her eyes on him.

He was so sure of himself, so confident as he took the cruiser toward the wharf. Kai told herself that nothing bad could happen to her as long as he was around to protect her. Even this afternoon, when he had jumped with her into the ocean, she hadn't been as afraid as she thought she might, with him beside her.

He'll make you a wonderful husband.

Oh, that inner voice of hers! She had to ignore it, throttle it, if she were going to have any peace. Still! It was fun, in a way, listening to it. It seemed to know more about her than she knew herself. But she had to be wary of it, too. Or she would be dragging Rod into her bed, rather than the other way around.

Kai smiled dreamily.

Then the cruiser was nudging the wharf and Rod was lobbing ropes over pilings. Kai stepped onto the wharf and ran to stand beside him, smiling up at him. She was hungry, she and Rod had both skipped lunch in order to enjoy their dinner all the more.

She caught his arm and walked where he led her.

The Coral Reef was a low, long building a block from the wharf. As they entered, they were met by the succulent odors of meat and fish, of shrimp and sauces. Kai felt her mouth water. Off to one side was a long bar, clustered about with men and women.

A girl came forward, smiling, a pair of menus in her hand. They trailed her between tables to a table set close by a window. Rod pulled out a chair for her, and as she sank onto it, Rod seemed almost to freeze.

Wonderingly, she glanced up at his face. He was looking at the bar. Kai turned her head, glanced at the men and women gathered there, sipping drinks and talking. Had he seen a gangster? The same man who had tried to kill her that time Rod had come swimming up to save her?

"Whom did you see?" she asked.

He gestured as he seated himself. "Just a friend. No one important."

"Rod, please! You seemed to change for a moment, there."

He smiled at her. "Now don't go getting excited. It's just an idea I got. Go ahead. Order a drink for you and a martini for me. I'll be right back."

He pushed back his chair and moved across the room. Kai stared after him incredulously. Who or what was so important to take him away from her? Ha! Maybe there was a woman there whom he knew, whom he was going to caution not to recognize him.

Kai scowled. Her eyes never left him as he settled himself at the bar alongside an absolutely gorgeous redhead. Jealousy and rage seethed in her heart. So! Him and his talk about not bothering with women! A big lie, all of it!

To her surprise, he ignored the redhead to talk to a bearded man in a sweatshirt and a pair of dirty dungarees. The man gave a bellow and caught Rod, hugging him. Then Rod was speaking to the man, conversing very seriously, very rapidly.

A waitress came up then and distracted her. Kai gave

their order for the drinks and then leaned on the table the better to get a look at the bar.

Rod and the bearded man were still talking. They had their heads very close together and seemed to be speaking in whispers. The redhead turned her head and studied Rod. Buzz off, sister. He's spoken for. Kai made a wry face. She had no claim on Rod. If a girl should take an interest in him, it was no affair of hers.

It's your own fault if it isn't.

Oh, shut up.

You could be engaged to him now, maybe even married.

Stop it! Stop it!

At least you wouldn't have to be jumping into the ocean every few minutes to stay calm. He would attend to that, if you were married.

Kai gritted her teeth, keeping her eyes on Rod. Ha! He was smiling now, nodding happily, patting the bearded man on the shoulder. The bearded man turned, saw Kai staring, and waved a friendly hand. Kai made a weak gesture with her own hand in return.

What had been so important that Rod had to go and talk to him? Leaving her sitting alone, like a wallflower at a dance! Irritation and anger moved up inside her.

"Who was that?" she asked coolly as he was seating himself.

"A good friend of mine. Professor Dan Middleton."

"Oh? And what was so important you had to rush off and talk to him about?"

Rod winked. "It's a secret."

Kai was opening her mouth to tell him she didn't like secrets when the waitress was back with their drinks. Rod caught his martini glass up and said, "To us. To our success."

He was so pleased with himself that she began to have second thoughts. If he was so delighted with what he had done, there was no sense in playing the outraged woman.

"Oh? A secret about what?"

Rod laughed. "About the weather. Middleton's a meteorologist at the university. But he's also a weather historian, you might say, for all of Florida."

Kai stared at him. "A weather historian?"

"Sure. Now maybe you can figure out why I wanted to talk to him so urgently."

She relaxed. "Oh! You want to make sure no storms or hurricanes are going to hit us while we're out on the ocean."

His eyes twinkled at her, but he didn't agree. Nor did he disagree, either. Kai told herself Roderick Grant could be a most annoying individual when he wanted to be. She took a sip of her piña colada and decided that it was not worth it to pick a fight with him. Let him have his fun.

Rod ordered two steaks when the waitress came again, and because their glasses were empty, another round of drinks. At Kai's uplifted eyebrows, he chuckled. "We are having a celebration. I think it only right that we drink to the dead and forgotten gods of earth.

"To the gods of storm, Adad and Marut and Teshup. To the gods of the sea, Ler and Poseidon and Aegir. Most especially to the gods of love, Eros and Aengus, Cupid and Bhaga."

Kai frowned. Was Rod trying to tell her something? She muttered. "What about the goddesses?"

Rod bent his head. "Forgive me. To Ino and Ran and Eurynome of the high seas, and to Venus, Hathor, and Freya, I offer salutations."

They sipped in silence when their drinks were before them, but Kai eyed him carefully over the rim of her glass. Suddenly she asked, "I can understand the toasts to the love gods and goddesses—but why toast the gods of storm and the seas?"

"Because we are going to sea and I want to placate them."

She did not believe him. He had some other reason for all this rigamarole. He was hinting to her. Oh, yes. Trying to convey an idea to her, to tell her something. Kai admitted she hadn't the slightest idea what it was.

Then the steaks were before them, with hot buttered rolls, tossed salad, and baked potatoes oozing with melted butter. Kai had never been so hungry, or so she felt. As her knife slid into thick steak, as she chewed upon that meat, she told herself that this was a foretaste of what life would be like, were she to marry Roderick Grant.

Traveling across the ocean, swimming together in the waves, stopping to have dinner together in some restaurant such as the Coral Reef: These were things she would be doing if she were Mrs. Roderick Grant. Mrs. Roderick Grant? It had a nice sound.

Of course, if they were married, they would have no secrets from each other. Rod would have to tell her what he had been discussing so secretly with Professor Dan Middleton. She was positive it had to do with something other than the weather. They had been entirely too secretive, too earnest, for something as ordinary as that.

What could it have been?

Nine

THEY CAME OUT into the dark night under a canopy of brilliant stars speckling the sky. A cool wind was blowing in off the ocean, ruffling her skirt, causing her to move closer to Rod, to catch his arm in hers. Behind them was the sound of men and women talking, the smells of food, the clinking of dishes and glasses. Out here, on this momentarily deserted street, they walked alone.

Kai did not miss the people. She enjoyed being by herself with Rod. It was almost as though he were an extension of herself, in a sense. At least, this was the way she felt.

"Can you take the *Atlantis* out to sea?" he asked.

"Certainly. But what are you going to be doing?"

"Looking at maps."

She halted her steps on the wharf, compelling him to stop. "Maps?" She frowned. "I thought you knew these waters."

"I do. But there are other things maps may tell me."

His voice seemed almost to be laughing at her. No, not laughing at her, but laughing with her, inviting her to join him. Kai would have loved to join in that secret laughter, if she could see anything to laugh about.

"What other things?" she asked quietly, staring up at him.

"Things that needn't concern you until the proper time."

"I hate it when you're so mysterious," she announced.

He patted her hand that he had caught hold of without her being aware of it. "Indulge me in my little game. It helps take my mind off how gorgeous you are, how tempting."

Mmmmm. She didn't know whether she approved of that or not. It was fun to balance precariously on the very edge of surrender, to wonder if he were going to sweep her up and take her into his cabin to make love to her. Still! It might be safer to play his silly little game.

"All right. For now, I'll let you amuse yourself by being mysterious." Then a pleading note crept into her throat. "But will I like this game of yours?"

"You'll love it almost as much as you love me."

"Ha! That may mean I won't like it at all."

"Don't be mean. Wait and be patient."

Patience had never been one of her virtues. However, she would go along with him, at least for a time. It might even be that she would like whatever game it was he was playing. But she didn't like to be kept in the dark.

As Rod cast off the ropes, Kai started the engines, listening to their throb, their humming power. She swung the wheel, felt the cruiser move almost as though alive as it turned its nose into the surging sea waves. It was glorious to stand here at night, to sense the power of the ocean spreading away before the *Atlantis,* and to know that she and Rod controlled the means of traveling anywhere they wanted upon the broad Atlantic.

For half an hour she gloried in the stars, the ocean, the power of the cruiser. Then she began to wonder where Rod was and what he might be doing. Had he gone to bed, leaving her to pilot the boat alone? She doubted that. Where, then, had he gone to?

With grim determination, she switched on the automatic

controls. Rod was below deck, busying himself with something. But—with what?

She dropped down the ladder and made her way into the galley. Rod was sitting at a counter with some maps spread out before him. He was scrutinizing them closely, totally absorbed. Kai stared at him, puzzled. What could be so interesting about those maps? He must have studied them so many times he should have known them by heart.

Her presence must have alerted him. He looked up suddenly, the preoccupied look on his face giving way to a sudden smile. "Hi. Sorry I've been so rude. But these maps fascinate me."

"Oh?" Dubiously, she took a step into the galley to stand beside him. Her eyes searched the maps, but they told her nothing except that they were maritime maps of the Florida east coast and the waters that lapped its shoreline.

"Want to make us some coffee?" Rod asked.

"If you'll tell me what you're doing."

"Just as soon as the coffee is brewed."

Curiosity hurried her to the stove, turning on the gas under the percolator. Almost in the same motion, she reached for the coffee. As she measured it out she glanced at Rod. He was lost in his study of the maps, but occasionally he would look up and stare at the counter, lost in some reflection. Then he would bend over the maps again.

"Three hundred years is a long time," he said, almost to himself. "A lot can happen in that period."

"Men and women can live and die," she snapped. "Kingdoms can fall. Customs can change. Clothes can change. Three hundred years ago, nobody had a telephone or a radio, let alone a television set."

"What? Oh. Oh, yes." He grinned at her. "And coral reefs can take shape."

Kai stared. "Coral reefs? What are you talking about?"

"You're the captain of a Spanish galleon," he announced.

"I am?"

"You're caught in a storm, a wild hurricane. It drives your ship helpless before it, toward the coast of Florida."

Rod paused, fully turned toward her. "From the poop deck, you can see the Florida coast. Now jump ahead a few hundred years. Is what you saw from that poop deck the same as you could see today?"

Kai frowned. "Of course not. There will be changes. Maybe a lot of changes. Coral reefs will have formed over the years. Maybe you won't be able to see them, but they're there."

Rod nodded. "Right. That's the conclusion I've come to. You've been looking in the wrong place for your sunken galleon."

Kai felt her heart skip a beat. Excitedly she ran to Rod, sat down upon the bench where he sat, staring at the maps. "What do you mean? Go on, tell me! You have something in mind. What is it?"

"Hey, don't get your hopes up. Not too much, anyhow. But after talking with Morrison, I've decided you and your brother were hunting for the *Santa Maria Gloriosa* in the wrong spot."

"How do you figure that?"

His forefinger touched a section of the map. "There are coral reefs here. But they may not have been there three hundred years ago when the *Gloriosa* foundered. In that case——"

"In that case, the *Gloriosa* would have sunk further on, away from where we were looking."

"That's my guess. I could be wrong, probably am. But I figure it's worth a try. I've been thinking that for the next week or so, we ought to go looking for it. We don't have anything else to do to keep us busy." He paused, and his eyes began to twinkle. "Unless you change your mind about marrying me. Then we could go ashore, get married and——"

"Stop right there. Go back to hunting for the *Gloriosa*."

He was very close to her on the bench. As a matter of fact, she was squeezed up against him so that he must feel a good deal of her body. She didn't dare look at him, she kept her head down as if staring at the maps. She wasn't really seeing those maps, however; she was too aware of Rod and his nearness.

"You're mean," he whispered.

"No, I'm not," she breathed.

"You love me just as I love you, but you're too scared to admit it."

"I'm not scared," she muttered.

Oooooh, you big fibber! You are too scared!

He was hugging her with an arm. How had he managed to get that arm around her without her being aware of it? She felt her body yielding languorously to the pressure of that arm.

"We could have such a wonderful life together," he went on dreamily. "Being with each other day in and day out. Nights, too, of course. Nights when we would jump into bed side by side after a bit of canoodling, and then we would have all night long to make love and——"

"Stop," she pleaded weakly.

"Can't you see it? I can. Neither one of us has any clothes on and. . . ."

Kai lifted her head and glared at him. "Will you *stop* it?"

His blue eyes were so hungry! Yet so gentle, so adoring! Her heart fluttered and bumped, and she was getting weak all over. It was as though she were glued to the bench, glued to his strong body. That powerful arm of his was drawing her so tightly against him, she couldn't breathe.

She could not resist him. Vaguely, she understood that she did not want to fight him. Oh, let him kiss her. Let him hug her all he wanted. Her head fell toward him almost of its own volition.

His lips gripped hers, held them firmly, yet softly. Waves of sheer delight surged through Kai at this point, her head whirled, and her body became a quivering jelly. She lay against him, letting him know the feel of her breasts where they hardened against his chest.

She had to get hold of herself! Now! This very instant! Otherwise. . . .

"You do love me! I know it!" he exulted.

"No," she whimpered.

"You want me to take you into my cabin." His deep

voice paused, then went on, "You know what will happen then."

Against his mouth—he had never taken his lips from hers, which puzzled her, because they had been talking—she pleaded, "Rod! You have to be strong for both of us. Please!"

"How can I be strong when I want you so badly?"

"You have to be," she wailed.

"Why?"

"Be-because I'm not. Because I'm so w-weak."

The pressure of his arm eased a little. Kai began to breathe again.

"Then do you want me to lift and carry you into my cabin? To make love to you?"

Against his chest, she nodded her head. But very weakly. It was almost no nod at all, but he understood her gesture.

His lips roved over her forehead, her cheeks, her nose. "You don't know what you're asking of me, angel. But if you want me to—you do want me to let you go, don't you?"

Kai hesitated. Did she?

What was the matter with her? Of course she wanted him to release her, to get away from her, to give her a chance to get her emotions under control. Yet a part of her did not want to be freed, wanted instead to be borne aloft in his arms and taken to his cabin. What was the matter with her, anyhow? She was like a ship without a rudder, tossed this way and that by a wind over which she had no control.

"Please. Let go of me. Be strong for both of us."

How had she found the strength to utter those words?

"Coffee's ready," he said abruptly, and rose to his feet.

Kai felt cold all over. It was as though a part of her had removed itself from her body. She shivered and put her arms on the table, letting her head hang. How was she ever going to get through a whole week without giving in to him? To say nothing of a possible *two* weeks!

Then he was back, putting a mug of steaming coffee under her nose. "Drink that. I'm going up to the wheelhouse. You'd better go to bed."

He left the galley. She could hear his receding footsteps. Kai lifted the cup, sipped from it. The coffee was hot, warming, but inside her she felt cold. She was being unnatural, she told herself. Her place was with Roderick Grant, no matter where he might be.

There, you see? You've finally come to your senses.

"It's no fun," she muttered.

Well, you know what to do about it.

No. She would not. She could not. The best thing for her to do was run into her little cabin and slide between the sheets. Fall asleep. Forget Rod and his kisses, how heavenly it felt to be taken into his arms and devoured with kisses. Forget all that wonderful stuff and just go to sleep.

"How can I possibly sleep?" she wailed.

Kai pushed the mug from her, got to her feet. The *Atlantis* was rolling a bit now as it surged forward into some waves, but she made her way to the companionway and to her bedroom door. She opened it, went in, and turned on the light. She closed the door and began to sob.

Tears welled up into her eyes and trickled down her cheeks. She stumbled to the bed and flopped down on it, burying her face in the coverlets and letting the sobs come up from inside her, stronger and stronger.

She had had such a good life, diving with Ken. Why had Rod Grant had to come into her life? Worst of all, why did he have to be such a great guy? Why did she have to fall in love with him?

Desperately, she wanted to run up there to the wheelhouse, to throw herself into his arms, to beg him to stop the engines and carry her down into his cabin. Every atom of her being urged her to do it. Yet she went on lying here like a big lump, oozing tears and racking sobs and feeling utterly miserable.

After a time, she fell asleep.

Kai woke to morning sunlight blazing in through the porthole. She lay a moment, stirring slightly, completely comfortable. It was so pleasant lying here, so warm and almost voluptuous. She smiled to herself and opened her eyes.

She had fallen asleep last night in her Enka! It would

be all wrinkled, soiled! Kai turned over onto her back and stared up at the ceiling. So what if the dress was messed up? She had more important things on her mind than clothes.

The *Atlantis* was moving forward, though only at half speed. Had Rod steered her all night long? Was he sleeping now?

Kai sprang to her feet, began to disrobe. She had to go find him, make certain he was all right, that nothing had happened to him during the long night hours. Her hands reached for her swimsuit.

She ran out of her cabin, turning toward the galley. Rod was not there, nor was he on deck or in the wheelhouse. Yet the *Atlantis* was moving forward steadily, at half speed. Kai felt her heart contract. Where was he?

She sped down to his cabin, where she hesitated. Ought she to knock? Maybe he was asleep, and if so, she did not want to wake him. Her hand touched the knob. If she opened the door and he were standing there naked....

"Rod," she called softly, "Rod, are you all right?"

The door opened. Rod stood there in his swimming trunks, big and bronzed, smiling. "Good morning. I see you're all set."

Kai blinked. "Set for what?"

"We dive, right after breakfast. Or as soon after as is safe. I've finally figured out where the *Gloriosa* ought to be."

"Oh?" She felt excitement gather in her. Could he be telling the truth? As he knew it, of course; but the real truth might be that the *Santa Maria Gloriosa* lay on the ocean bottom miles away.

He took her arm, guided her along the companionway to the galley. "I've done some hard thinking during the night, considering the maps and the way this coastline was about three centuries ago. I don't think the *Gloriosa* would be as far north as you and Ken were looking.

"It should be farther south. As a matter of fact, not far from where we are now."

She had to use willpower to keep her voice from betraying her gathering excitement. "Then you're going to dive?"

"So are you. Two people can explore more territory than one. You might see what I might miss."

Kai did not want to dive. She still feared those green depths and what might be hiding down there. Her common sense told her they were far away from where that man had sought to kill her, but the fear persisted. She hurried from Rod's side to open the refrigerator door and remove bacon and several eggs.

She had to fight that fear, defeat it. Common sense told her that a killer who would be swimming around looking for victims back where she had been attacked would not be here, waiting for her. That was simple logic.

She stared down at frying bacon, arguing with herself. She had to dive. She *had* to. Rod would be down there with her, he would protect her if anything should happen. She was not going to spend the rest of her life out of the water. No way.

And yet. . . .

The memory of that moment when she had thought Rod was trying to kill her surfaced strongly. She had not seen the man Rod had driven away. Now she believed him, though. If Rod had said a man was there, a man had been there.

She shivered. She had to be brave, she had to ignore her fears, to recapture those moments of swimming far down on the ocean bottom when she had enjoyed them, had lived for them.

Her eyes went sideways toward Rod where he was making toast. She had to be brave, for his sake. It was something he expected of her, and she could not disappoint him.

No matter what might happen.

Ten

OVER BREAKFAST, ROD began to talk.

"I mentioned those coral reefs last night. My theory is that the *Gloriosa* passed over what is now an outer reef and that the winds of the hurricane drove it further on, so that it sank beyond it."

He shrugged, took a sip of coffee. "I could be wrong. I'm the first one to admit that. But I have a gut feeling about it. Then, too, I feel that the galleon wouldn't have been driven so far north. It would be in water somewhere along Key Largo."

Kai made a face. "That's a lot of territory to cover."

"We don't have anything pressing us for time. So how about it? We'll make dives and travel northward as we do. Sure, I know. You feel it's like hunting for that proverbial needle in a huge haystack. But we can have fun doing it, can't we?"

She shrugged. "Why not?"

At least, it would give him something to think about other than how much he loved her. Maybe he would lose some of his energy. Ha! Maybe she would, too. If they

139

could exhaust themselves by swimming all day long, they wouldn't have any energy left to make love. Right?

"We'll take our time," Rod said. "We'll do the dishes, get into our gear, then drop overside. We'll make an exploratory swim, at first, just moving along easily. I've made a sort of grid map to help us cover as much of the sea as we can."

Two hours later, she was swimming past coral formations, watching starfish move past her, flipping their tails almost flirtatiously, seeing crabs scuttle out of the way as she glided above them. An ugly fish moved into view. Kai gave it a glance, then swam upward and away from it, recognizing the Caribbean scorpion fish. If it had touched her with its venomous spines, she would have regretted it.

She saw coral reefs and scarlet gobies flitting in and out of them. There were little schools of grunts moving in and out of the gently waving fronds of a flexible coral called sea fans. Off to one side she saw a group of jacks easing their way past a section of staghorn coral.

It was a wonderworld of color and movement through which she glided. For moments on end she forgot about the *Santa Maria Gloriosa*, lost in the gliding beauty of a small barracuda as it coasted through a clump of sea grass. Down here in the quiet of the sea, a person was alone, cut off from the rest of the world.

A shadow touched her, made her look up. Rod was there, swimming steadily, motioning to her to extend her search. She gave him a flip of the hand and swung sideways, swimming off into another corner of this undersea world.

The chronometer on her wrist told her that she would have to surface, to swim to the *Atlantis*. She would have to replace her oxygen tank. When she came up into the air, Rod was about thirty feet away. He began swimming toward her, came up with her when she was within a few feet of the boat.

"No luck," he said as he helped her up onto the deck. "We'll move on, try again."

"I think it's hopeless," she murmured.

"Hey, don't despair." A shadow touched his face as he

asked anxiously, "Aren't you enjoying it? If you're not, you stay on board while I dive."

Kai shook her head. "Oh, no. We're in this together."

Besides, she added to herself, if she got tired enough, she wouldn't be in any mood to have him kissing her. She wondered if he ever got tired. Maybe all the exercise only gave him more energy.

All that afternoon they swam beneath the surface, gliding in and out of coral formations, disturbing any number of fish, yet seeing nothing that looked the slightest like a Spanish galleon.

For the next three days they moved steadily northward, always diving in the morning and in the afternoon. Kai was getting very discouraged, she was beginning to think that there had never been any such ship as the *Santa Maria Gloriosa,* though she knew differently. If the galleon was down there on the ocean bottom, it was well hidden.

One thing their swimming did accomplish, though. Both she and Rod were tired at the end of the day. Each late afternoon she just about was able to drag herself up on the deck, to sprawl out and let the sun dry her while she regained a little of her strength.

They would eat their dinner, talk a little, then go into their bedrooms for their much-needed sleep. Kai would strip off her swimsuit, don a pair of pyjamas, and slide between the sheets. She was no sooner covered than she fell into a sound slumber.

The days passed and became a week. They had explored so much of the ocean bottom that she felt she knew it by heart. Yes, and all the coral reefs that lined this part of the coast.

Then came the day when Kai said over breakfast, "I'm beat. You go down today, Rod. All I want to do is laze in the sun."

"Oh, come on. It's no fun swimming by myself. Besides, we're in a corner of the world we've never searched before. The *Gloriosa* may be down there. If I were to find it, think how rich I'd be. I could keep its location to myself and come back here and become a multi-billionaire."

Kai laughed. "If you find it, it's all yours."

"Oh, no. Half is yours. Actually, a third. Because we'd have to give a third to Ken."

She stared at him. "That's very generous, but how do you figure that out?"

"He let me bring you with me, didn't he? I owe him."

Kai sniffed. "Ken isn't my keeper. What he says doesn't influence me."

Rod leaned forward, eyes glowing. "Aha! So now you admit it! You were ready to come along with me of your own free will."

She scowled. "Just to avoid being killed."

His expression was rueful. "Is that the only reason?"

He looked so disappointed that Kai shook her head. "No, it isn't the only reason."

"What, then?"

Kai shook her head, smiling at him. "You don't think I'm going to tell you, do you? A girl has to keep some secrets."

How could she tell him that she had fallen in love with him, and that she wanted to be with him just as much, if not more, as he wanted her with him. Thinking back, Kai admitted—to herself, that is—that she may have fallen for him when he carried her off to his Everglades cabin.

His eyes lighted up and he rose to his feet. Something in Kai warned her that she must be on her guard. If he grabbed her now, there would be no diving today for Roderick Grant. She lifted her hands toward him, palms up.

"Down, boy! Stay away, Rod. Remember, you're going to dive in a few minutes."

He drew a deep breath. Slowly, he exhaled. "You're right. I do have to dive, don't I? But one of these days. . . ."

His eyes glowed, and Kai shivered, delighted at what she could see in them. She told herself to look away, not to gaze too deeply into those blue eyes, or she would be completely lost.

"I have to do the dishes," she yelled, jumping to her feet and gathering dishes and coffee mugs in her hands. "Go put on your diving equipment!"

She retreated before him, dishes and mugs a barrier between their bodies. She went backward until the sink was against her. Rod still stood as he had been standing, eating her with his eyes, seemingly poised on the very verge of leaping after her to hold her close.

"You right, of course," he said slowly. "I have the diving to do. But don't you ever break down? Don't you ever listen to your heart? To your emotions?"

"That's why I'm so afraid of you," she whispered.

"If I didn't consider myself a gentleman," he muttered, "I'd. . . ."

"Go diving," she breathed. "Please, Rod?"

He nodded slowly, turned on his heel, and walked to the companionway. Kai let out her breath. Wheee! That had been a close one, there. If he had come toward her and taken the dishes and the mugs out of her hands, if he had put his hands on her, she would have melted.

She would have run with him into his cabin, raced to the bed and leaped with him upon it. Oh, yes. She knew that, now. Nothing could have saved her.

What are you scared of? The guy wants to marry you.

"We aren't married yet," she said to herself. "And who can marry us out here on the ocean?"

Hurriedly, she began to wash the dishes. Anything to keep from thinking, to keep active, to do something—anything!—that would prevent Rod from getting too close.

She was drying the dishes when Rod called from deck. "I'm going down, now. You want to see me off?"

She ran from the galley out into the sunlight. Rod was poised on the edge, ready to go over, fitted out with his aqualung, his air tanks, his goggles, and his mouthpiece.

"How about a kiss for luck?" he grinned.

Kai walked forward, "Keep your hands by your sides!" she warned.

She leaned forward, pressed her mouth to his, then gave him a shove. He bent over backward into the waves. Kai felt her heart contract and stepped to the edge, peering down.

Yes, he was all right. He was waving a hand up at her, then turning and going downward. She watched until he was out of sight, then turned and spread out her towel on the deck. She would doze here, get some sun. Rod would be back in a little while.

She fell asleep, stretched out comfortably.

She dreamed, lying there. She was swimming along with Rod in and out of huge coral growths, without any diving equipment on. As a matter of fact, she didn't even have her swimsuit on. She was naked and Rod was naked too, though she didn't dare look. But he was chasing her.

When he caught her, he was going to drag her into his coral castle where he had a bed, where he would make love to her. She was swimming only half-heartedly, wanting him to catch up to her. What was delaying him? He could swim faster than she, and she wasn't making any great attempt to get away.

She turned and saw a huge whale right above her. The whale had seen her, was coming down toward her. Its bulk filled the ocean, huge and black and monstrous. It was going to land on her!

She turned onto her back, lifting her hands to try and keep that weight from crushing her. It was no use. The whale was too heavy. It dropped her, she felt its weight on her stomach, heavy and wet. . . .

Kai screamed.

Her eyes snapped open. Rod was standing above her, grinning down at her. But she still felt that weight on her stomach!

"Sorry," he said, "I didn't mean to scare you."

"It was just a dream. Sorry to be such a sissy."

Something was heavy on her stomach, though. Even if she was awake. Almost wonderingly, she put her hands to her bare middle, felt something smooth and shaped in a rectangle. Her hands went around it and she lifted it up.

Her eyes went wide. She was holding something yellow, something heavy. Her stare went to Rod, who was laughing almost hilariously.

"Rod!" she squealed, sitting up and staring at the gold bar. "Is it real? Where did you find it?"

"Not going to tell you."

Her mouth dropped open. "You're not?"

"Going to show you. Come on!"

His hand caught hers, lifted her to her feet. She ran to

where her diving equipment lay, began to slide into the straps. Rod was there, helping her.

"Tell me, tell me," she babbled. "Is it down there? The wreck of the *Gloriosa*? Is that where you got the ingot? Oh, come on, Rod. Talk!"

He shook his head. "No, I'm going to show you what you missed by not diving with me this morning."

His hand gripped her, drew her to the gunwale. They sat on it, they went over backward. Down they went, downward, with Rod swimming beside her, pointing, guiding her. Through the sea-green water they swam, side by side.

She saw a cannon first, covered with barnacles, and then her eyes beheld what was left of the *Santa Maria Gloriosa*. It was half-buried in sand, but she could make out what was left of its bulwarks, the masts that were snapped off. Everything was encrusted in barnacles, but she knew inside her that this was what she had been searching for, for so long.

Rod tugged her, drew her with him toward a hole in the hull. Kai swam with him, paused at the opening in the waterlogged wood. There was little light down here, but she could make out the shape of chests. Some of them were broken open and spilling from them....

Gold! Gold in ingots, lazily gleaming.

Light came suddenly from a lamp Rod was carrying. That light streamed in over that long-lost treasure room, making the gold glint in yellow splendor, drawing colored sunbursts from jewels that were heaped here and there in tiny piles.

Kai stared. She could hardly breathe as she hung here in the opening. She was looking at untold wealth, at gold and jewels that had not seen the light of day for centuries.

Blindly she reached out, caught Rod's hand, and squeezed it tightly. Her heart felt as though it were leaping up into her throat, and tears came into her eyes. A hand pushed her gently and she swam forward into that treasure room, trying to look everywhere at once.

Rod touched her arm and when she turned he was holding out a red jewel to her, balancing it on his palm. Her eyes grew big when she saw how large it was. Rod was putting it into her hand, closing her fingers over it. It was a ruby, she understood that, a ruby of fabulous size.

Then Rod was moving away from her, lifting a diamond, an emerald. These he passed to her, then swam further and gathered up several gold bars. He swung about then, pointing upward.

Kai nodded, turning, and swam out of the wreck, rising toward the surface. She still could not comprehend it all. It seemed almost like part of that dream she had had before Rod woke her. Yet the ruby in her hand was real, she could feel it by squeezing her fingers around it. She was rich. Rich!

Hey, wait a minute. It was Rod who had found the treasure. By right, it belonged to him. Yet he had said he would share it, if ever he found it. She wanted to call out to him, to make certain of this. But he was swimming toward the *Atlantis,* and Kai wanted very much to be with him.

He was waiting for her at the ladder. Kai pulled the mouthpiece from her lips and asked breathlessly, "Was it real? Am I dreaming, Rod?"

"Let's see," he chuckled.

His arm went around her and held her close. Ha! She should have known what he was going to do. But she did not care. In fact, she wondered why she had not thought of this. His mouth came down on hers and her lips rose to meet it.

They hung on to the ladder, kissing, half floating in the ocean, being lifted and rubbed together by the waves. Her lips fell apart, she knew the touch of his tongue upon her own. Slowly, she bit it; not hard, just enough to tease. A love bite.

When they broke apart to breathe, Rod asked, "Were you dreaming that?"

"I'm not sure," she giggled. "Let's try it again."

Ooops! That was a mistake. Because Rod's arm about her yielding middle grew stronger, clasping her against him so closely that she knew he could feel every curve of her body. She could feel his body, too, come to think of it, and that touching was setting off rockets deep within her.

When he let her speak, she breathed, "It was no dream, that's for sure."

"So let's go up there on deck, and prove it some more."

He swung her about so that the ladder was before her. Kai went up it, still clinging to the big ruby. Her head was whirling, she felt light and airy. Something was happening to her and she did not know what it was. His hands were on her, pushing her upward.

Then Rod was standing behind her, loosening straps, removing her diving gear, lowering it to the deck. He was also divesting himself of his own equipment, she saw. Next moment he would be taking her into his arms.

She opened her hand and saw the ruby for the first time in open air. It was huge! She had never seen a stone quite as big. Its blood-redness mesmerized her, kept her eyes glued to it.

"It's magnificent," she whispered.

"Take a look at this," Rod chuckled.

He was holding out a diamond so blue-white that where the sunlight hit it, it seemed to sparkle. "It must be ten carats at least," he was saying. "It'll make a perfect engagement ring."

She raised her eyes to his. "Engagement ring?" she asked weakly.

"For you, silly. Of course, the engagement will be rather short because the marriage is going to take place just as soon as I can get you before a preacher."

Tears came into her eyes. "Ohhh, Rod."

He nodded. "That's right. Just as soon as we can get back to port. Meanwhile, here's some more loot."

He poured half a dozen diamonds, mixed in with a couple of emeralds, onto her outheld palm. Kai stared down at those jewels, still not quite believing that they were real.

"I need a drink," Rod announced. "A great big one. How about you?"

Kai nodded, telling herself that a drink would calm them, would let them relax. It never occurred to her that liquor, on top of this elated feeling that held her in its grip, might be a dangerous combination.

Eleven

WITH A HAND at her elbow, Rod escorted Kai down into the galley, where he reached under a counter for a bottle of Chevas Regal. Kai eyed the golden liquor, telling herself that she had to be careful, she did not have a head for liquor. Still, she did not stop him when he began to pour the scotch over ice cubes.

Rod lifted his glass after handing one to Kai.

"To our success as treasure hunters," he announced.

She took a sip.

"To our future happiness together as millionaires."

Kai swallowed some more Chevas Regal.

"To our love."

Kai obediently drank some more.

The liquor was warming. It was smooth to the palate and the taste buds, it slid down her throat and heated up her insides, giving her a rather mellow outlook on life in general and her life in particular.

She smiled up into Rod's face happily, telling herself that she was a lucky girl. Oh, more than lucky! She was a favorite of the gods. Here she had a man who wanted to marry her, and a fortune in gold bars and jewels lying down there under the sea, waiting for her to come and get it.

She and Rod were the only ones who knew the location of the *Santa Maria Gloriosa*. It was like having a secret bank account in Switzerland. Any time they needed money, all they had to do was come out here and get it. She smiled even more, and when Rod put an arm about her to hold her close, she leaned into him.

Who couldn't be happy with all that?

"That was just to coat our stomachs," Rod was saying, taking her glass from her fingers.

He was refilling his glass and adding more ice cubes. Kai was vastly surprised to discover that her glass was empty. Ah, but not for long. Rod was filling it again and handing it to her.

Then he was touching his own glass to hers, whispering, "To the most beautiful girl in the world."

"I can't drink to that," Kai objected with a giggle.

"I can," Rod nodded, and took a long sip.

"However, I can drink to the man I love," she went on, tilting her glass.

"You're not just saying that?" he asked softly.

"Sure I'm saying it. You see anybody else around here who could have?"

Rod was closer than ever, an arm gripping her middle. "I think that calls for a kiss."

Kai told herself that was a wonderful idea. She lifted her mouth to his, felt his lips crush hers—but gently—even as his arm strained her body to his own. A tiny voice whispered to her that this might not be such a good idea, mixing drinks and kisses, especially with Roderick Grant. She was discovering that she could not hear that warning voice very well, probably because of all the Chevas Regal she had swallowed.

She was absolutely boneless. Rod was hugging her more firmly, now—he must have put his drink on the counter, because he was using both arms to hold her— and she was discovering that her almost naked body was having strangely agreeable reactions.

There was a little bomb in her middle that was exploding every other second, sending warm waves of delight throughout her flesh. She was quite certain that she had never experienced anything quite so pleasurable. Oh, sure, she had loved it when Rod had kissed her at other times, but right now his kisses were igniting fires in her every nerve end.

She was actually pushing her body into his, moving a little so that the pleasure of their contact was increasing. Her breasts were warm, her nipples were hardening, and her middle was feeling all mushy. If she didn't stop soon, she would be unable to stop at all.

Rod was whispering against her lips.

She had to concentrate to make certain she would understand what it was he was saying. And who wanted to come out of this blissful Nirvana into which she had collapsed to listen to words? Still, she felt she had to concentrate. A little, anyhow.

" . . . love you more than life. Love you even more when you're my wife, even if I can't see how that will be possible. All I'll do when we're married is worship you. Adore you. . . ."

He would have gone on like that endlessly, she knew, if she hadn't kissed him with her open mouth. Lazily. Hungrily. Trying to tell him soundlessly that she felt exactly the same toward him as he was saying he felt toward her.

She put both arms about him, gripping him. And that was strange, because she had a glass in her hand. Or she had had. Rod must have taken it away from her. Good for Rod! How could a girl hug her man with a glass of scotch in her fingers?

His hands were sliding all over her, gently, caressingly. He was touching her bare back, moving over her bikini-suited buttocks, as though urging her even closer. Ha! She couldn't get any closer. She was right up against him so that her curves were blended with his hardness.

It seemed to Kai that they turned together, almost at an unheard signal. Still clinging, they moved from the galley out to the companionway and along that to his cabin. From moment to moment, as they walked, they paused to kiss and cling to each other.

Then they were both staring at the bed, standing together.

Hands were at her back, undoing the bra part of her bikini. As it fell away, she lifted her arms, then let them drop. No! Suddenly, Kai wanted him to see her, needed to let him know how firm her breasts were, so hard they almost hurt. As he stared worshipfully, she slid down the bikini panties.

After that. . . .

Kai could never remember clearly just what did happen. She knew only that she was lifted high in his arms, carried to the bed, and that Rod dropped down beside her. Yes! And then he began to kiss her, not just her lips but her entire body, hungrily, almost as though he were devouring her.

She was raised high on an incredible wave of utmost bliss. She shuddered and clung to him, knowing that this was her man, the man to whom she belonged. This was right and proper, this was heaven on earth.

Kai lost all track of time.

Later, she opened her eyes, and knew that she had drifted off into sleep. There was a warm body against which she was cuddled, there was an arm about her, and her head was nestled on a male chest.

She smiled a little, stirring. Oh, not moving away. Oh my no! She was just getting closer. Closer, all the time closer, so that she might almost become a part of this man named Roderick Grant.

Then she drifted off to sleep again.

A kiss woke her. She smiled lazily and returned it, whispering, "I'm absolutely shameless."

"You're going to be my wife," Rod was murmuring gently. "We're going back to town and get married, but that's only for appearances."

"Will Ken ever be surprised!"

"Not really. He knows how I feel about you."

"He does?"

She knew amazement, wondering how her brother could have known. She hadn't told him, never even hinted. Of course, she had loved Rod, but back then, the last time she had seen Ken, she hadn't realized it. Maybe it had showed, though. It must have, if Ken had known about it.

"What about Sandra?" she asked slowly.

"What about her? She knows I never loved her. Personally, I think she and Ken are probably hitting it off, right about now."

"You think so?"

"We'll know soon enough. I'm taking the *Atlantis* in. We've been gone long enough for Bill Trent to have learned something."

Kai shivered and crept closer, knowing the comfort of Rod's arms about her, holding her. "Do we have to go back?" she murmured.

His kiss covered her mouth. "Only to get married. Then we can come back out here for our honeymoon." He hesitated. "That is, unless there's somewhere else you want to go."

She shook her head. "This is heaven. I don't want anything else. Just you and me together."

He was turning her, drawing her beneath him, and Kai went very willingly. Eagerly, as a matter of fact.

It was dark when Kai woke a second time. She knew, as soon as her eyes opened, that Rod was awake, just holding her close and waiting for her. She stirred against him, whispering, "You know something? I'm starved."

"I'm hungry myself. We skipped lunch."

Kai giggled. "For more important things."

"How does steak and onions sound to you? Plus buttered toast and maybe a small helping of french fries?"

"It's the only thing that could get me out of your arms."

"You take a shower while I go get things ready."

Then he was off the bed and moving wraithlike through the dark cabin, pausing only to snatch up a pair of shorts and slide into them. Kai lay a moment longer, savoring her happiness.

Was it true? Really true? Did Rod actually love her as much as he claimed? Did he really want to marry her? She felt a desperate need to run to him, to get him to tell her all over again how much he adored her, how much he wanted to make her Mrs. Roderick Grant.

Yes, she would do that. But only after having showered and put on something slinky and tempting. Hmmm. No, better not do that. They had to eat dinner, and she had the gut feeling that they might skip dinner also if she made herself too enticing.

Kai slid from the bed and ran for the shower.

In her room, she donned shorts and a blouse, but fussed with her hair, fixing it so that it hung about her face in a brown aura. She touched her lips with dark red Givenchy lip gloss. As she eyed herself in the bureau mirror, she had to admit she looked pretty good.

Rod was frying sliced potatoes and grilling a steak. He turned and stared, his eyes wide, and Kai felt herself rewarded for the care she had taken to make herself look appealing.

"You're even more beautiful than I remembered," he whispered.

"Silly! I've been away from you for less than fifteen minutes."

"I know. That's what I can't understand. How can you have become even more gorgeous in such a short space of time?"

Laughter grew within her, and she had to resist a very definite desire to run forward and throw herself into Rod's arms. Kai compromised by blowing him a kiss. Then she came toward him, hitting him with a hip and taking the stirring fork from him.

"You go sit down. Let me handle the rest of this meal."

He stared down into her brown eyes. Kai wished he wouldn't do that, it turned her into something between a love-hungry tigress and a lovesick teenager. All she could do was stare back at him, eating him with her eyes.

"We have to stop this," she whispered.

"I know. But I can't help it. I just love looking at you."

"You know what will happen," she breathed.

Rod grinned. "I sure do."

He took a deep breath. "I'm trying to bolster my willpower. To look away from you, to go over to that toaster and take a couple of slices of bread and insert them into it."

"Go do it. Please!"

"Okay. At the count of three, we each turn away. One. Two. Three."

They turned, but glanced back at each other and burst out laughing. Rod lunged for her, caught her, and kissed her, then thrust her toward the stove. "There. That has to hold us—at least until after dinner."

Kai smiled and nodded, but there were tears in her eyes. How could any girl be so lucky? Rod was something she had never even dreamed of, in all her years. She had never believed a man such as he existed, let alone that she would meet him and that he would fall in love with her.

If only there was nobody wanting to kill her! How happy she could be! But that danger was present, it was waiting for her—somewhere out there on the ocean. Or under it.

Kai shook her head. Forget the danger! Enjoy these moments. Concentrate on cooking this succulent steak and frying these potatoes with the onions mixed in with them. She bent her head and paid attention to what she was doing.

Rod opened a bottle of wine, poured the burgundy into two glasses.

Then they began to eat. Kai was discovering that she did have an appetite, after all, and that Rod seemed equally as hungry. Of course there were moments when they paused in their eating to eat one another with their eyes, to reach out and hold hands.

"Can it always be like this?" she wondered.

"We'll make it so," he nodded.

Over their coffee, Kai asked, "Are we going back the way we came? Up the international waterway?"

"It'll take us too long. No, I'm going to strike out straight for home."

Kai frowned. "What about those men who fired at us?"

Rod shrugged. "It's night. I think we'll be safe enough. What I'm most concerned about is whether Bill Trent has learned anything. If he knows who shot at us, who tried to kill you, it'll be a big help."

She thought about that. "By morning we ought to be docking. All right. I vote we try it."

"Good girl. I'm going up on deck. Leave the dishes and come with me. We'll share the run together."

Kai rose, began gathering the cups and dishes, putting

them in the sink. Rod helped her, his face grave. She studied him when she was sure he was not watching, knew that he was worried. Well, why shouldn't he be worried? Killers were out there on the Atlantic, probably keeping an eye out for anyone who should come along.

Rod waited for her, went with her along the companionway and out onto the deck. The sky was flooded with stars, but there was a moon. A velvety blackness covered the lifting waves, forming a shrouding darkness through which they would travel. Except for their riding lights, they would be invisible.

Kai went up the ladder to the wheelhouse, watched as Rod sat himself behind the wheel. A touch of his hand and the twin diesels throbbed to life, purring smoothly. He gripped the controls, swung the *Atlantis* northward. She sat right behind him, her eyes roving out across the water.

For half an hour they traveled steadily northward.

Kai sat quietly, hands clasped, watching Rod. He was in complete control of his boat, there was no hesitation in him. He did not have to glance at charts, now. He seemed to know instinctively just where he wanted to go.

It was dark out here on the ocean, so black that they could see nothing at all except an occasional glint of starlight on the waves. Yet even that light vanished after a time, as clouds rolled across the sky. It was as though they were cut off from all humanity.

When she spoke, her voice seemed very loud. "Rod, where will we live after we're married?"

He turned his head, smiled. "On campus during the school year. I have a condo there—living room, den, two bedrooms, a couple of baths. It's been too big for me, living alone, but for two of us, it's perfect."

"It sounds like a good life."

"It's perfect. I like the atmosphere and you can't beat the hours. I lecture and teach about eight hours a week. The rest of the time is my own. Our own, now."

"You'll want to go on teaching, even after finding the *Santa Maria Gloriosa?*"

His chuckle was soft in the darkness. "For a time, anyhow. I wouldn't know what to do with myself, not having young people to teach. Hey. You have any objection to that?"

"None at all. I think it sounds wonderful. Though I am wondering how I'll fit in with the faculty wives."

"Not to worry. They'll take you to their hearts. They've all been after me to get married, anyhow. I guess they feel a professor ought to be old and crotchety, married and tied down to some good woman."

"Tied down?"

"You know what I mean. There's always talk about an unmarried professor and his female students."

Kai sat up straighter, frowning slightly. "Oh?"

"Sure. The married girls are all trying to get the unmarrieds hitched. I think they've just about given up on me, though."

"What about these female students?"

"There have been a couple who sort of cozied up to me, but when that happened, I always ran off to the Everglades to give them a chance to cool down."

"Hmmmm. I'm getting the feeling that the sooner we're married, the better it is for both of us."

"Hey, now. Don't go getting suspicious. Those kids don't mean a thing to me. Never have. I just keep them at a distance."

"You'd better go on doing just that, Roderick Grant," she caroled happily. "But then, I'm going to keep loving you so much you won't have any energy left to fool around."

She leaned forward, putting an arm about him.

It was then that a bullet clipped the woodwork of the wheelhouse.

Twelve

KAI SCREAMED. SHE could not help it, that keening cry came up from deep inside her, shattering the stillness just as had the bullet. She fell off the chair and into Rod's arms as he whirled to hold her.

"Are you all right?"

She nodded. "Yes. I th-think s-so. It w-was so sudden!"

His hands pushed her down on the wheelhouse deck. At the same time he turned and, gripping the wheel, pushed the speed of the *Atlantis* to its limit. Almost at the same time, two more bullets hit the framework of the wheelhouse.

Instantly, Rod dove to extinguish all his riding lights.

In complete darkness, the cruiser surged forward through the waves, heading eastward now, straight out toward the vast Atlantic. Rod was at the controls, silent and grim. More shots rang out, but none of them was even close.

From where she crouched at his feet, Kai could sense the powerful motors as they revved up to full speed ahead. The cruiser was leaping forward, seeming almost to relish this display of power. Faster it went, ever faster. Invisible in the dark night, she fled from her attackers.

For half an hour she raced across the water, shedding the waves at her bow, and then—suddenly—Rod shut off the power.

Silent now, the *Atlantis* rocked to the motion of the waves. The night was still around it, quiet. Yet it seemed to Kai as she huddled close to Rod's knees, that she could hear the running of a ship's engines.

Rod knelt down beside her, whispering, "They're trying to catch us, but they don't know where to look. We're just a dark blob on the water. They'll never find us."

Kai wished she could believe him, but her heart was hammering so loudly, her mouth was so dry, that she could think of nothing but her terror, of the fact that men wanted them dead. She moaned a little, shivering.

"Easy, now. Easy."

It seemed to Kai that she could see light. She lifted her head, peered. Yes! There was a searchlight out there, scanning the waves. Yet it was far away. And it seemed to be receding, even as she looked.

Breathlessly, they waited, with Rod holding her close. His arms about her eased some of her fears, his warmth quelled her quivering coldness. It was good to be held this way by the man she loved, even if there was danger out there. Kai rested her head on his shoulder and clung to him.

Time went by slowly in the darkness.

After a while, Rod got up, drawing her with him. Together, they peered out the wheelhouse windows, seeing nothing but darkness, hearing only the waves pounding the hull and lifting the *Atlantis* only to lower it again in the trough.

"What are we going to do?" she whispered.

"Wait. Wait for an hour or two, until those bastards figure they've lost us. Then we can go on."

"Will it be safe? Won't they hear us?"

Rod was silent for a moment. Then he said, "I don't believe so. They'll figure they've lost us. I doubt that they'll stay around until daylight, searching. Still, we'll

160

travel without lights for a time, just to be on the safe side."

"Why, Rod? Why are they trying to kill me?" she wailed.

"I haven't the slightest idea. You're the only one who can answer that."

"But I don't know!"

"Hey, don't worry. Come morning, we'll be docking, and then we'll get in touch with Bill Trent. He'll send a police car for us. All we have to do now is just keep dark and keep silent."

"Can they hear us talking?"

"Not if we keep our voices down."

Kai moaned, "Just hold me, then."

The minutes dragged on. From time to time, Rod would glance at his wristwatch, but it was too dark to see its numerals. He leaned against the wheelhouse side, holding Kai to him, occasionally kissing her forehead, her cheeks.

She gathered strength from him, nestling closer.

It was almost annoying when he pushed her back and away, saying, "We can go, now. I doubt very much that anyone has waited this long for us to make a move."

He started up the engines and turned the *Atlantis* west and north. Kai stood beside him, her nervousness still ran strong inside her, together with her fear; she did not want to stir even so much as a foot away from Rod. She felt safe with him.

In a way, that was strange, because she had never been afraid when by herself, before now. It was as if, having yielded to her love for him, she was bound to him in some invisible manner. Once she might have hated this dependence, but now she found herself glorying in it.

All through the rest of the night they stood close together, watching the waves fall away behind them. Steadily, the *Atlantis* slid through the ocean waters, moving always west by north.

There was no more gunfire. It was as Rod had said: Their attackers must have lost them, then turned away to move homeward themselves. Yet Kai could not quite believe this, always her eyes searched the dark waters as if expecting the ship that held those killers to loom up out of nowhere.

Dawn found them sliding by Miami Beach, with Golden Beach dead ahead. It was a clear, lovely day, with no trace of clouds in the sky. Soon now, they would be docking, they would be phoning Bill Trent. Danger was a thing of the past.

"We'll make our phone call, then have breakfast," Rod told her, smiling down into her upturned face. "By the time we've eaten, Bill ought to be there."

"I'm not hungry," she murmured.

"You will be. What happened tonight will slide out of your memory. You have to go on living, you know. I want a live girl as a bride."

Kai smiled and leaned into his arm. "I guess I'd better eat, then."

They docked at a marina, and walked along a sidewalk until they came to a restaurant. When they walked past it, Kai looked at him in surprise.

"Phone booth on the corner. We have to make that call first."

She crowded into the booth with him, watched as he dialed, then listened as he asked for Lieutenant Trent. After that, when Trent got on the line, all she could hear was Rod.

"We're back, we're going to eat breakfast at the Golden Spoon, Bill. I hope you'll send a police car for us . . . you will? Good. Incidentally, we were fired on last night as——"

He broke off, listening. Then: "Yes, it was about the same spot as those other attacks took place. Okay, okay. I'll fill you in later. Be seeing you."

Rod hung up, opened the phone booth door.

Kai asked, "Well? What did he have to say?"

"There's been another murder. One of Dolly Donati's boys. Donati's wild, half out of his skull. But Bill says he's been a lot of help—whatever that means. But right now we're going to forget all about that and have us a big breakfast."

"I don't think I can."

Yet when she was inside the Golden Spoon and sitting

at a booth, Kai felt her appetite stir and come to life. Eggs with bacon began to look good. And the coffee which a waitress poured out for them as soon as they were seated, tasted delicious. For the first time in a long while, she was more relaxed.

"If only we could get this over with," she murmured.

"It can't go on forever," Rod assured her. "Besides, if nothing happens, we're going back into the Everglades for our honeymoon. Then when it's all settled, we can return to a normal way of life."

Kai shrugged. "I surely hope so."

They lingered over breakfast, each reluctant to return to the business of helping Lieutenant Trent. They had more coffee, they sat and talked about their future plans. Kai frankly admitted she didn't have any plans, except to get married. Rod told her his only plan was to make certain that her life was safe.

A shadow touched them. As they looked up to see Bill Trent standing beside their table, the police lieutenant said, "Must be nice, running off by yourselves while everybody else is working hard to save your life, young lady."

Kai laughed. "You can't make me feel guilty, lieutenant. Rod and I are getting married."

Bill Trent cuffed Rod on the shoulder. "Move over, man. I guess I can spare five minutes to offer my congratulations. So. You've both finally seen the light."

Kai raised her eyebrows. "I beg your pardon?"

Trent chuckled. "Anybody with half an eye could have told you that you two were crazy about each other. Ken knew, even Sandra realized it."

"Oh, did she?" asked Kai.

"She sure did. Now she's changed her sights and is in love with your brother."

"She isn't!"

"Sure is. And Ken's nuts about her. We may even have a double wedding. How about that?"

"Sounds fine to me," Rod nodded. "But right now I'm more interested in making certain that Kai stays alive."

The police lieutenant rubbed his chin thoughtfully.

"Well, now. About that. We have to catch those killers before that can happen."

Rod stared at him. "I know you. You have something up your sleeve. Come on, spit it out. What's on your mind?"

But Bill Trent only shook his head. "Can't tell you now. Or rather, I won't. I have a meeting set up in my office in about half an hour. Just enough time for us to get there so it can get started."

"What kind of meeting?" Rod asked suspiciously.

The officer grinned. "Tell you when the time comes. Now let's move it."

They followed him out to the police car, with Kai sitting in the front seat between the two men. She felt very subdued. She had not liked the sound of Bill Trent's voice, she had not liked his hint. He had something in mind which she was not going to be glad to hear. But what could it be?

Bill hit the siren and they went through traffic and red lights at eighty miles an hour. Ordinarily, she might have enjoyed this sensation, but right now, Kai began to get the idea that she was being rushed to her own execution. There was an old adage that bad news always travels fast, but Kai felt there was no reason to break speed limits to get to it.

As they walked into Trent's office, the first person she saw was Dolly Donati, sitting on the edge of a chair and nervously drumming his fingers on its arm. To one side of him, on a couch, Ken was sitting, with Sandra Alberts close beside him.

"About time," Dolly snapped, but his nervousness seemed to ease slightly.

Ken got up and moved toward Kai, taking her in his arms and hugging her. "You're still alive, anyhow," he grinned.

"Yes, and if I go on living, Rod and I are getting married."

At that, Sandra let out a squeal and ran to Rod, throwing her arms about him and pressing up against him to kiss him. Kai felt jealousy stab all through her, she broke free of her brother and was about to speak when Ken pinched her.

"Relax, sis. Sandra and I are getting hitched, too. She's just an emotional person, she likes to let people see how she feels when she's happy."

Sandra was whirling then, grabbing hold of Kai. "We're going to be sisters! Isn't that wonderful?"

Her animosity melted away as she hugged the other girl. "Great! We'll have fine times together."

There was a babble of talk until Bill Trent pounded his desk.

"Hey! Hey! Let's have a little less levity here. We got business to talk about."

Kai went and sat in a big armchair, with Rod perched on its arm. Sandra and Ken resumed their seats. Dolly Donati looked from one to the other of them, his face cold and hard.

"This ain't no family celebration," he muttered.

Bill Trent announced, "We've done a lot of work in the days you were away having a good time. We know now that a gangster named Cheeks Tegrino has come down into Florida with the idea of driving Dolly here out of business. He's been murdering his boys and getting rid of their bodies in some way we haven't been able to figure out."

"Me, I don't care about that," Dolly snarled. "I'm going to give Tegrino all he can handle."

"Dolly, you made me a promise," Trent protested.

"Sure I did. But what have you done? Nothing!"

"These things take time."

"I'll give him and his boys concrete coffins, that's what I'll do!"

Kai gasped and sat up straight, her eyes wide. Her gasp was so loud that everyone turned and looked at her.

"I forgot," she breathed, and turned to Rod. "Oh, Rod—I'm so sorry!"

He gaped at her. "Sorry? About what?"

"Aflantis! I would have told you. Really, I would! But I've been so happy with you, I just never gave it a second thought!"

Rod shook his head. "You've lost me, angel. I haven't the slightest idea what it is you're babbling about."

"That stone wall I saw under the sea. That time we went swimming together with Bill and Sandra and Ken on the boat. Remember? When those men shot at us?"

"I remember the time, yes. But. . . ."

"Well, when I was swimming, I saw those concrete blocks—long things, they were—part of a wall. A wall of some Atlantean building, Rod! It proves you were right. There *are* Atlantean ruins off the Florida coast."

Kai did not notice Bill Trent glance at Dolly Donati, eyebrows raised, nor did she see Dolly quiver and lean over farther from his chair. Twice the gang boss licked his lips before he spoke.

"Concrete blocks?" he rasped. "Where, for God's sake?"

Kai looked at him. "Under the sea, where Ken and I were diving to try and find the *Santa Maria Gloriosa*. Oh! I forgot again. Ken—Rod and I found it!"

"What?"

"We found the treasure!"

Ken was off the sofa, kneeling before Kai, gripping her hands, looking from her to Rod and back again. "What's this? What did you say?"

Kai fumbled in her handbag, brought out the immense ruby Rod had given her. "Not only this. Look here!"

She brought out a little bag, upended it so that a shower of rubies and diamonds fell into her cupped hand. The light caught those jewels, made them scintillate and glow.

Even Dolly Donati was awed. He rose and stood staring down at those gems, seeming scarcely to breathe. Sandra was beside him, her mouth open as she gaped. Ken was frozen speechless.

"Show them the gold bar, Rod," Kai laughed.

They stared at the gold, back to the jewels.

Rod said, "We're splitting our find three ways. A third to Kai, a third to Ken, a third to me. There's plenty down there for all of us."

"I'm in the wrong business," Dolly murmured.

Only Bill Trent did not seem impressed. He sat at his desk, arms resting on its surface, eyes staring straight ahead. His lips moved, but no sound came out. He was scowling, but as he sat there, his scowl evaporated and a look of utter contentment came into his eyes.

His eyes turned toward the little circle of excited people. He began to grin.

Kai was smiling up at Sandra. "You can't have the ruby, Sandra—that's mine, a gift from Rod—but you can have any other jewel here, as Rod's and my wedding present."

The golden goddess squealed and looked at Ken, who laughed and gestured. "Go ahead. Pick out one. I'll give you another one from my share." He looked at Rod. "You're sure about what you said, Rod? About giving me a third?"

"You bet I am. You'll never have to ask Sandra's father for any money with your share of what's down there, just waiting for us."

"Can you find it again?"

"No problem. As a matter of fact, Kai and I are going to spend our honeymoon down there on the ocean floor, scooping up all that treasure."

"Hey! Sandra and I will help you. How about it, my lovely one? You game?"

Sandra's eyes glistened with happiness. "Am I ever! You bet!"

Bill Trent cleared his throat. "If you rich folk are finished gloating over your gold and jewels, can we get down to business?"

Sandra and Ken returned to their seats. Dolly Donati shrugged and sat down. Kai began to return her jewels to her handbag.

The police lieutenant leaned forward over his desk. "Dolly, I know where your boys are buried."

The gangster leaped from his chair, crying out, "You know? But you said you didn't. Are you playing games with me, lieutenant?"

Trent chuckled and shook his head. "No, Dolly, I'm not. It was Kai Pierce who told me."

Dolly whirled on Kai, eyes wide. *"You?* You know?"

Kai gaped, gasping, "What are you talking about? I don't know a thing!"

"Oh, yes you do," Trent smiled, leaning back in his chair.

Kai turned and stared up at Rod, who was scowling at his friend.

"Is this some sort of joke?" Rod asked.

Bill Trent shook his head, all the while looking at Kai. He was waiting, patiently.

Thirteen

THERE WAS A silence in the room. Kai could hear the others breathing, she could even hear herself as she drew air into her lungs. Her eyes went from the police lieutenant to Dolly Donati, then to Ken and Sandra, at last to Rod who was glowering at Bill Trent.

"I don't know anything," she wailed.

"Sure you do. You told me, just a few minutes ago. Think, girl!"

Kai licked her lips. "All I did was show the jewels. . . ."

"Before that," Trent grinned.

She thought, sitting there, her handbag clasped tightly in her hands. "I mentioned that stone wall I saw, evidence of Atlantis——"

"Atlantis!" Trent snorted. "It was no more evidence of Atlantis than this desk I'm sitting at." He leaned forward, eyes intent. "Describe what you saw, Kai. Please!"

She closed her eyes, to give her memory a better chance. Once again she recalled how it had been, swimming along, seeing those long, rectangular stone slabs as they had lain on the ocean bottom, seemingly tossed about as though a mighty force had smashed them, thrown them helter-skelter here and there on the sands.

She spoke softly. "I saw a wall, obviously a very ancient one since it was so far under water. Atlantis is supposed to have been destroyed by a mighty earthquake, or a series of earthquakes—perhaps caused by something like a vast meteor out of space...."

"Phooey," said the police lieutenant. He turned to Dolly Donati. "Dolly, what do you say?"

The gang boss spread his hands. "What do you want me to say? I know nothing about this Atlantis."

"Those things aren't part of Atlantis, or any colony of it. They're something else."

Donati stiffened. His eyes went wide. He shouted, "Coffins! Concrete coffins!"

Lieutenant Trent slapped his desk top. "Now you've got it! Now you know where your boys are. Under the sea. Now we know why Kai was shot at, why somebody wants to prevent those coffins from being found."

Kai gasped. Rod was on his feet, excitement making him nod his head. "Sure. It all adds up."

Dolly Donati was quivering. "At last. Now I can order out my boys and go get that Cheeks Tegrino!"

"How will you do that? You don't know where he's hiding."

"I'll find him," Donati announced grimly.

"Sit down, Dolly. I have a better idea. We're going to make him come to us."

The gangster stared. "Oh, sure. How we going to do that?"

Trent pointed at Kai. "That little lady is going to help us."

"Oh, no!" Rod shouted. "You're talking about my future wife. She's not going to dive to make those hoods come out of hiding!"

Kai shivered. The mere thought of going into those ocean depths again, near those cement coffins, was enough to freeze her where she stood. It had even been a little hard for her to go down to view the wrecked *Santa Maria Gloriosa,* and there had been no one around her there except for Rod. But to go diving again, especially where one of those murderers might be waiting for her!

She just couldn't!

And yet, even as her eyes met those of Lieutenant Trent and saw the appeal in them, as she turned to see Dolly Donati hanging on her words, she realized that she had to make the effort. To let more men be murdered by this Cheeks Tegrino was utterly unconscionable.

She would be protected, she felt sure.

Her tongue moistened her lips. Almost in a whisper, she said, "I could give it a try."

Rod turned to her, scowling. "Kai, you're putting everything on the line! Our love, our marriage, our future life together."

"I have to," she whispered to him. "Can't you see? If people like us won't help the law, who will? I must dive again. I must!"

He took her in his arms, held her tightly. Against her hair he breathed, "I'm proud of you. By God, I am! But I'm going to make sure nothing happens to you."

Rod turned to Bill Trent. "All right. She dives—but I dive with her, and I'm going to carry an underwater gun, Bill. Nothing's going to happen to her. Nothing!"

"You think I want anything to happen? If you do, you're crazy. She's going to be protected every step of the way."

Dolly Donati came forward, tears in his eyes. "She will be safe, believe me! My own boys will be there, along with the police."

"Dolly, I can't permit that," Trent rasped. "But I'll have enough men on board the *Atlantis* to make certain she's well protected. And you can't bring your own boat out. That would tip our hand. Can't you get that?"

The gangster swung around, rigid. After a moment, his anger faded and he nodded. "Yes, you're right. We have to catch Tegrino, I don't want him to get away. But I'm coming. I'll be on this *Atlantis*. Is it agreed?"

The police lieutenant sighed. "Okay, okay. I can make that concession." He turned to the others. "When do we dive?"

Rod smiled. "Whenever you say."

"This boat of theirs patrols those waters. My men have seen it. If we prepare to dive—it's only a few minutes past eleven now—we can lure them out, I'm sure."

Ken said, "We'll drive you to the *Atlantis*. We'll go aboard and then Rod can take her out."

Trent reached for a phone. "It's settled, then. Just wait until I can call my men. I'll have them on the *Atlantis* inside half an hour. They'll get down below decks, out of sight."

They waited while he gave instructions, Rod standing with an arm about Kai, holding her tightly, while Ken and Sandra conversed in whispers. Only Dolly Donati moved about the room, walking in short steps, muttering to himself.

Then they walked out into the morning sunlight, moving toward Ken's car. Kai sat in the back with Rod and Dolly, while Bill Trent slipped into the front seat with Sandra and Ken. Ken drove smoothly, easily, in no hurry, aware that the police needed time to board the *Atlantis* and get out of sight.

Kai was trembling slightly. Despite her rash promise, she knew that she was terrified. Going down there along the ocean floor with a killer hunting for her was going to take all her nerve, her bravery. Her hands held Rod's, she leaned against him, wondering if he would be able to keep her alive.

The *Atlantis* seemed deserted as Ken swung the car in close to the dock. There was no sign of any police, but Bill Trent seemed confident that they were aboard. Rod walked with Kai, with Trent and Dolly ahead of them and Ken, with Sandra, bringing up the rear.

Rod left them then, to check his oil gauges, to start up his twin diesels. Kai came up on the wheelhouse deck with him, standing close.

"You're not to worry," he told her. "I'll be with you, and there will be a lot of cops here to make certain that nobody on that other boat will be able to shoot you when we come to the surface."

Kai shook her head. "I'm not worrying about that as

much as I am about somebody down there." She nodded her head at the ocean.

"I'll be carrying an underwater gun," he growled.

"Make sure you see him first." She half smiled.

"Count on it. I'm protecting the most valuable girl in the whole world."

She leaned into him and he kissed her.

Bill Trent called up to them. "My men are all aboard and safely hidden away. Any time you want, Rod, get going."

Rod reached for the throttle.

As they moved outward, Kai let her eyes roam the ocean. It seemed bare of ships, only the sunlight danced across the waves. She had to stay calm, she scolded herself. No nervousness—at least, none that showed!—and above all, no hysterics. She had a job to do, she wanted to get it done the best way possible.

It seemed no time at all before Rod was turning, calling to Ken to join them, asking him to take over the controls. As Ken came up, Rod nodded to him, and then guided Kai toward the steps.

"Time to get into our swimsuits," he told her.

Kai gave a little smile to Sandra as she went past her, with Rod at her side. Sandra looked frightened, tense, and her eyes stared at Kai almost in awe. Bill Trent was somber, grim, and Dolly Donati had moved to the rail, where he leaned, his eyes intent on the water all around them.

Only when she moved into the companionway and saw the policemen, each of them armed with submachine guns, did she realize how serious this was. She stumbled slightly, but Rod had a good grip on her arm.

As he opened the door to her cabin, they saw there were more men in there, armed and quiet, waiting. Rod chuckled. "Guess we'll have to use my room, if I can chase the boys out. Get your things, Kai."

He went into his room, where more men were sitting or standing. "Sorry, boys. We have to get ready."

When the room was empty, save for themselves, Rod whispered, "Okay. Climb into your gear. I'll be right outside the door."

Kai wanted him to stay, but she realized that they had to keep up appearances. After all, she wasn't Mrs. Roderick Grant yet. As soon as the door closed behind him, she stripped off her blouse and shorts, reached for her bikini. Then she was sliding into the back pack, strapping her diving knife to her leg, lifting the regulator and depth gauge.

She moved out into the companionway on trembling legs, making her way past Rod and the policemen, moving toward the stern. Rod went into his room to get ready.

Lieutenant Trent met her as she emerged into the sunlight, a worried expression on his face. "You all right? You sure you want to go through with this?"

Kai nodded. "I'm sure."

She stared out over the waves. There was a boat a long way off, but it seemed to be coming toward them. She glanced at Bill Trent, who nodded.

"Unless I miss my guess, that's the one." He glanced at Dolly, who had been staring hard at that boat. "How about it, Dolly?" he called.

"She's almost exactly like my old *Napoli*. Maybe it is the *Napoli*. Somebody bought it. I've never been able to find out who." He slapped his palms together. "My new boat—the *Hurricane*—is very much like it, only bigger. That bastard Tegrino must have bought it."

"We'll know soon enough," Trent nodded.

Rod came on deck, fitted out for diving. He lifted an aluminum air cylinder and fitted it to Kai's back pack. Then he glanced around him. "We're almost there, everybody."

Trent nodded. "You dive. I'm staying here. As soon as I see any activity on that other boat, my men will come up shooting."

Kai fitted on her fins and walked with Rod to the rail, leaned her rump against it. Ken was slowing the *Atlantis*, they were almost over the spot where they would dive.

"Another two minutes," Ken called from the wheelhouse.

Then it was time. Kai felt for Rod's hand, caught it,

squeezed and was squeezed. She went over backward into the ocean, with Rod beside her. She sank downward, turned and was swimming. The water was clear, she could make out the sandy bottom, grew aware of a sea urchin drifting past, the silvery shape of a flounder, and off to one side, the momentary blur that was a bluefish seeking its prey.

She swam steadily, forging ahead with a steady pumping motion of her fins. Somewhere around here were those concrete coffins. Kai turned her head this way and that, seeking them. One glance behind her told her Rod was covering her, but swimming above and behind her. She hoped he wouldn't let himself get too far behind her.

Kai moved over a sandy hummock, then found a coral growth beneath her. Those coffins had to be somewhere nearby. She swung sideways to the coral, moved on.

That was when she saw movement up ahead of her.

A man was coming straight at her, a harpoon gun in his hands. He was coming swiftly, intent on her as his prey. To one side of him, she saw the piled-up concrete coffins.

Terror caught her in its grip. Fear was a tide of utter helplessness flooding all through her. One tug of that man's finger on that harpoon gun and a length of lethal steel would go right into her!

Kai swung about, rising upward.

She saw Rod go tearing past her, swimming furiously. Something shot between them, barely missing her. The harpoon! Kai closed her eyes spasmodically, then opened them, turning her head to stare where Rod was swimming.

He was closing in on the man with the harpoon gun. A knife was in his hand, just as a knife was in the hand of the other man, who had dropped the harpoon gun.

No, Rod! No! Let him go! Don't. . . !

The silent scream came up inside her, shaking her entire body. Rod was locked with the man in a furious struggle, their bodies were twisting and turning, as each sought to break free of the other in order to stab with the knives they held.

For an instant, fright surged through Kai, urging her to flee upward, toward the open air and possible safety. Instead, she swung about and swam toward the two men. Almost unbidden, her hand went down to her knife.

She had to help Rod. She had to! She must fight to keep him alive!

Kai tried to get close enough to use her knife, but their bodies moved so swiftly she was behind the attacker at one moment, then in back of Rod. She felt utterly helpless.

She had to do something! She couldn't let Rod get hurt.

Kai swam forward, right at the attacker. He saw her, he drew back. Just for an instant, his attention was diverted from Rod. In that moment, Rod struck. His knife drove forward, sank to its hilt in the belly of the other man.

The attacker fell away, blood streaming from his wound. Rod let him go, turning toward Kai and pointing upward.

Kai let her eyes touch the man who had fired at her. He was helpless, bent over, clutching his midsection. He would be no more a threat. She began to kick, swimming upward.

Side by side, she and Rod headed for the surface. As her head popped out of the water, she heard gunshots. Off to one side was the *Atlantis,* its rail crowded with policemen armed with submachineguns, firing steadily. Three hundred yards away was another boat, the men in it firing back.

Even as they watched, the other boat began to turn, to flee.

The *Atlantis* went after it.

Kai took the breathing tube out of her mouth. "Rod, they've forgotten us! They're going after those killers!"

Rod swam closer, until he could touch her. "Relax, honey. They'll be back. Right now it's more important for them to catch up to that boat, to capture those men."

"What about us? We're all alone out on the ocean!"

The ships drew away, moving faster and faster.

Kai felt deserted. No matter where she looked, all she

could make out were the surging waves of the Atlantic Ocean.

Would she and Rod drown out here? Already, she was feeling cold.

Fourteen

KAI CLUNG TO Rod, whimpering. The touch of his body helped, it seemed to warm her. His arms about her were protective, as though telling her that with him beside her, there was nothing to fear.

But she was afraid. That fight down below, the strain of having had to dive again, were taking their toll. She shivered and trembled.

Rod said, "Relax. Help is on the way."

"Oh, s-s-sure. Easy to-to s-s-say."

His smiling face was before her. How could he smile at a time like this? He asked, "Don't you hear it?"

"Hear w-what?"

Ah. Now she could make it out. A humming sound, a steady roaring. Chopper blades? Kai lifted her head, looked skyward.

Yes! There it was, like some magnificent friendly bird, swooping down on them. A police helicopter! It was slowing, beginning to hover. A hand tossed out a rope ladder. The whirly bird lowered itself until the ladder dragged the waves. Then it began to ease forward slowly, bringing the end of the ladder skipping across the water.

Rod caught hold of it. "Up you go, honey."

"I don't know whether I have the strength left," she muttered.

But she did. Once those rope crosspieces were in her hands, she tugged on them, feeling Rod push from below. Rung by rung, she went up the ladder until hands appeared in the open doorway of the chopper, gripping her wrists and swinging her up and into the cabin.

Rod was right behind her, stepping into the cabin and reaching for a blanket that lay on one of the seats, wrapping it about her. She sighed and relaxed, her head on his shoulder.

There were two men in the chopper, the driver and an assistant. They were both grinning, nodding at Kai and Rod. "Thanks to you, lady, we've got those guys," the driver said.

The helicopter rose into the air, moved forward.

Almost in moments, they were overtaking the *Atlantis*. Looking down, Kai could see Rod's cruiser overtaking the other vessel. The shooting seemed to have slackened off, only an occasional burst of gunfire from the *Atlantis* sounded now.

"We've got 'em," the man beside the driver said, peering downward. "More than ten of them down—wounded or dead. The others are raising their arms, surrendering."

"Thank God," Kai breathed. "It's all over."

The driver turned his head slightly, saying, "We're going to put you down on the *Atlantis*. You ready?"

As she set foot on the deck of the cruiser, the first thing she saw was Dolly Donati's scowling face. He was pacing up and down, snarling to himself.

"What's wrong?" Kai asked him.

"Cheeks Tegrino, that's what's wrong. He ain't on that boat!"

Kai stared. "His men will be able to tell Lieutenant Trent where he's hiding."

Dolly sneered. "You think they'll rat on him?"

Bill Trent was worried, too, she could see. He was scowling, watching his men board the other boat, leaning on the rail with Rod at his side.

"Tegrino will run," he was saying. "He won't stay around Miami any longer, waiting for us to find him."

Kai could see Dolly shaking his head. "Not yet, not yet. He's got something to do," he was muttering. His black eyes fixed on Kai speculatively.

What could this Cheeks Tegrino have to do? His try to run Dolly Donati out of town was broken now by the police. There would be murder warrants out for him, once those cement coffins were brought up.

When she said something of this to Donati, he shook his head. "You don't know Cheeks like I do. The man will be crazy. He'll want revenge."

"Revenge? For what?"

Those black eyes bored at her. "For you showing up his neat little scheme, lady. He'll be out to get you, and get you good."

He turned away even as cold terror struck through Kai. Wasn't she ever going to be free of this business? Was she going to be followed to be killed the rest of her life? She walked toward Rod.

He turned as she approached. "Hey, honey. Better get into some warmer clothing. Come on, I'll go below with you."

When they were turning into her room, Kai said, "Rod, I'm scared. Dolly claims this Cheeks Tegrino is going to kill me for what I've done."

"What? He's off his rocker!"

"I hope so. But he claims Tegrino is very vengeful, that he won't run—not yet. Not until he pays me back for what I've done to him and his dreams of empire here in Miami."

"I'll talk to Bill. Meanwhile, you get dressed. You're shivering, you're so cold."

He kissed her and closed the door. Hurriedly, Kai slid out of her swimsuit, donned a sweater and slacks. Warmer now, she hurried out onto the deck. Dolly Donati was talking with Lieutenant Trent, waving his arms and arguing, though in a low tone.

Then Rod was emerging from the companionway, clad in slacks and a short-sleeved shirt. He came to her, drew her toward the wheelhouse ladder. "Let's go relieve Ken. He's been up there for a long time."

Ken and Sandra smiled at them. "You okay?" Ken asked.

"So far. What are we going to do now?"

"We're heading back to where you dove. The lieutenant wants to get one of those coffins up on deck."

"I'm not diving again," Kai yelped.

"Easy, now. The police have divers who will do that. As a matter of fact, by this time there are men diving right now, I should imagine."

Sandra and Ken left the wheelhouse. Kai crowded close to Rod, murmuring. "That gangster scared me, Rod, talking about how Cheeks Tegrino wants revenge on me."

"I know. But you aren't to worry."

"Not worry! Are you out of your mind?"

"Bill knows all about it. We're going to be guarded day and night. Meanwhile, Bill will try to learn from the captured gangsters where this Tegrino is hiding out."

Kai clasped her arms together. She didn't like this new development, not at all. It was bad enough to be shot at while under the sea, but to have to try and avoid being killed on land was too much!

She stayed by Rod's side all the way back to where she and he had dived. There was a police boat there, together with a diving boat, and she could make out chains running downward into the ocean.

"They're attaching chains to one of those concrete coffins," Rod told her.

Kai shivered, feeling a desire to turn away. She could not, she had to know. It seemed forever before the waves broke and she made out one of the concrete lengths being lifted upward, shedding seawater as it came. Horror touched her, as she realized that there might be a body inside that thing.

What kind of man was this Cheeks Tegrino? He lacked a soul, she thought, and was utterly callous as to what might befall his fellow man. A murderer, surely, who would have no compunction about killing. Who might even look forward to it, as a fisherman might look forward to hooking a fish. Ah, but what a difference!

Rod was patting her hand, saying, "Relax, honey. You'll be protected. Nothing's going to happen to you."

Oh, sure. That was easy to say. But all a man had to do to kill her was point a gun at her—and fire. All the protection in the world couldn't save her when that happened. She nestled closer to Rod, felt better as his arm slid about her, gripping her closely.

The concrete coffin was swung over to land with a slight thump on the deck of the *Atlantis*. Men were bending over it with jackhammers in their hands. The racket deafened her as those drills bit into the concrete. Kai turned her head away, stared out over the waves.

She waited, scarcely breathing.

Then there was a muffled curse, a babble of voices. Men crowded around that length of concrete, and she could hear Dolly Donati's voice ring out as he cried, "That's all that's left of Benny Gee!"

"You can identify him?" Bill Trent asked.

"Of course! Benny and me—we been friends all our lives. He always wore that ring you see on his pinky. I gave it to him. And that scar on what's left of his face—saw him get that in a fight when he was a kid."

Lieutenant Trent nodded. "Okay. I've heard enough. I'll get the necessary papers out when I get back to the office. Right now I want to bring the rest of them up." He turned and came over to where Kai and Rod were standing.

"We'll be here a little longer. You two can go back, if you want, but I'd rather you stayed on here." The lieutenant's face grew hard. "It's safer."

Rod smiled grimly. "We'll stay, Bill. We're going down into the galley and make some sandwiches and hot coffee. You and your men will need them."

Kai found she was very grateful to Rod for his suggestion. She was happy to be anywhere but up there with that stone coffin and what was inside it. She almost ran into the companionway and the galley, then rushed to the refrigerator to take out packaged slices of meat.

Rod said, "Will you take it easy? Nothing's going to happen to you now."

"That other man—that Cheeks Tegrino—is still free,

isn't he? Didn't you hear what Dolly said? He'll blame me for what happened."

Rod dug his hands into his slacks pockets. "He'll be so busy running away, he won't have any time for you—even if he knows about you."

"Oh, he'll know. That boat of his will have radio communications on it. His men will have been in touch with him. They'll know about me."

Rod took her in his arms, turning her away from the counter. He held her very tightly. "You'll be safe. I promise it. Now, just take it easy."

It was easy for him to say, Kai thought. Still, the feel of his body against hers, the grip of his strong arms holding her, reassured her. She took a couple of deep breaths, and smiled up at him.

"Right you are. Life must go on. Now we've got to feed those men and give them some coffee."

Time moved swiftly after that. Before she knew it, the concrete coffin was being transferred to the deck of the police boat, and men were gobbling up her sandwiches and gulping her hot coffee. She even managed a nibble and a sip herself.

Then Bill Trent was saying, "Okay, you folks can go in, now. I'm going back on the police boat, with Dolly." He cleared his throat. "I want to thank you for everything you've done. We couldn't have solved this case without your help."

"I just hope it doesn't cost me my life," Kai muttered.

"You'll be protected, believe me."

Worry lay in her eyes as she watched Bill Trent drop down into a tender and be conveyed toward one of the police boats. With him and the policemen went her protection, she thought. True, Rod and Ken and Sandra were still with her, but against a man like Cheeks Tegrino, they might not be enough to keep her alive.

Kai went up the ladder to stay close to Rod as he swung the *Atlantis* toward land. She wished they were heading anywhere but toward Miami. Cheeks Tegrino was there, and he would be furious. She remembered that Dolly Donati had said that even Cheeks Tegrino did not war on women. Still, she was not any too sure about that.

Rod took his time, almost making certain that the police boats should beat him in. When Kai commented on this, Rod shrugged. "I'm not in any particular hurry. Are you?"

"No. No, of course not. I could stay out here with you forever. Hmmm. Speaking of that, why don't we?"

Rod turned, caught her and drew her in against him. He kissed her hungrily. "I want to marry you, you sweet darling. The sooner the better. Have you forgotten that?"

"Mmmm, no. But——"

He kissed her again. "Just relax, angel. Plan our wedding dinner. How many people do you want to come to it?"

Kai smiled. "Just you and me. Oh, yes, Ken, too. And Sandra. We'll need a bridesmaid and a best man, won't we?"

It was dusk when they eased the *Atlantis* in against the pier and Ken and Rod affixed the ropes to the piles. Lights were on in the taverns, in the restaurants. As they walked toward Ken's car, Kai felt Rod's hand catch hers and hold it.

"We'll go to your place first," Rod was saying. "Then we're going out to dinner."

Kai looked at him in surprise. "My place?"

"Sure. To let you freshen up."

She frowned. It seemed to her that she and Rod would be a lot safer running off to the Everglades. Cheeks Tegrino didn't know about that hideaway. She would be very safe there.

Still! It might almost postpone the inevitable. If that gangster really wanted to kill her, he would stay on in Miami, hidden in some out-of-the-way place, ready to pop out and shoot her whenever he got the opportunity....

Almost in a daze, she climbed into the rear seat with Rod. She sat very close to him, aware that he was putting his arm about her and holding her. Ken was starting the car, Sandra with him in the front seat.

Ken drove slowly through the gathering night. They were silent in the car, no one was saying a word. Like that, they drove through the old, familiar streets until Kai could make out her house. Ken slowed even more, pulled into the driveway.

Sandra got out, with Ken. Then Rod was stepping out, giving Kai his hands and helping her from the front seat. They all walked toward the door.

"Okay, lady! This is where you get it!"

Kai whirled, seeing a man crouched low beside some bushes where he had been hiding. There was a submachinegun in his hands, and he was grinning coldly.

The world erupted, then. Guns began to chatter all around her as Kai stood mesmerized, aware that Rod was in front of her and Ken was joining him. Off to one side, she could see Bill Trent and Dolly Donati, together with half a dozen plainclothesmen, each of whom were firing.

Cheeks Tegrino was dead, standing there. His weapon drooped, slid from his fingers even as he himself started to fall face first onto the ground. Kai stared at him, frozen motionless, unable even to scream.

Then Rod was whirling, yanking her against him, squeezing her. "It's over, honey—all over! He's dead and you're safe."

Dazedly, Kai saw Bill Trent coming toward them, his face grim. "We thought he might come here, so we came here too, right from the dock. He's dead, Kai. You don't have to worry about a thing from now on."

She looked up at Rod. "Did you suspect he would be here, too?"

Rod looked embarrassed. "We talked it over, Bill and Ken and I. We decided we had to take the chance." He frowned down into her face. "Maybe we should have told you, but we were afraid you wouldn't consent."

Dolly Donati came out of the shadows. He removed his hat and made a little bow to Kai. "It was for the best, lady. We had to bring Cheeks out into the open. Knowing him, I was sure he would try something like this. But now you're safe, now you can marry your gentleman—and I hope you'll be happy ever after."

Kai sighed. She could not be angry, a wave of such relief flowed through her that all she was able to do was cling to Rod and look about her, tears in her eyes—happy tears—and a smile on her mouth.

"I want you all to come to our wedding. You, Bill. You, Dolly. I won't consider myself married unless you agree."

"Count on it," Bill grinned.

"It will be an honor," Dolly chuckled.

Then they were gone, and Kai found herself alone with Rod. Even Ken had disappeared, with Sandra. And Rod was staring down into her eyes with worry in his own.

"Will you forgive me?" Rod was whispering. "I felt it was best for us."

Kai wound her arms about his neck. "There's nothing to forgive. I might even have volunteered, if I'd known about it. But you have to promise me one thing, Roderick Grant."

He smiled and kissed her. When he could, he asked, "What do I have to promise?"

"No more secrets. Never! When we're married, we're like one person."

"Agreed, agreed. That's just the way I want it."

Their kisses went on for a long, long time.

More Adventures in Love from SIGNET

                                                          (0451)

- ☐ **ALOHA TO LOVE** by Mary Ann Taylor. (087658—$1.75)
- ☐ **HAWAIIAN INTERLUDE** by Mary Ann Taylor. (090314—$1.75)
- ☐ **BON VOYAGE, MY DARLING** by Mary Ann Taylor. (116666—$1.75)
- ☐ **BITTER HONEY** by Hermina Black. (116631—$1.75)
- ☐ **DANGEROUS MASQUERADE** by Hermina Black. (116623—$1.75)
- ☐ **LOVER'S REUNION** by Arlene Hale. (077717—$1.50)
- ☐ **STORMY SEA OF LOVE** by Arlene Hale. (079388—$1.50)
- ☐ **HOLD BACK TOMORROW** by Anne Starr. (110331—$1.95)
- ☐ **COME KISS A STRANGER** by Anne Starr. (113608—$1.95)
- ☐ **THE LOCH** by Janet Caird. (116658—$1.75)
- ☐ **CHARADE OF LOVE** by Sharon Wagner. (112865—$1.95)*
- ☐ **AMETHYST SUMMER** by Claire Cameron. (114698—$1.75)

*Prices slightly higher in Canada

Buy them at your local bookstore or use this convenient coupon for ordering.

THE NEW AMERICAN LIBRARY, INC.,
P.O. Box 999, Bergenfield, New Jersey 07621

Please send me the books I have checked above. I am enclosing $_____
(please add $1.00 to this order to cover postage and handling). Send check or money order—no cash or C.O.D.'s. Prices and numbers are subject to change without notice.

Name_____

Address_____

City _____ State _____ Zip Code _____

Allow 4-6 weeks for delivery.
This offer is subject to withdrawal without notice.